Across th

A Novel

By Nora Ryan

© Copyright 2002 Nora Ryan. All rights reserved.

No part of this publication may be reproduced, stored in a retrieval system, or transmitted, in any form or by any means, electronic, mechanical, photocopying, recording, or otherwise, without the written prior permission of the author.

This book is a work of fiction. Names, characters, places, and incidents either are products of the author's imagination or are used fictitiously. Any resemblance to actual events or locales or persons, living or dead, is entirely coincidental.

Cover design by Cathi Stevenson BookCoverExpress.Com
Cover photo by Robert Cortright Bridge Ink

National Library of Canada Cataloguing in Publication

Ryan, Nora
    Across the great divide / Nora Ryan.
ISBN 1-55369-680-8
    I. Title.
PS8585.Y359A73 2002   C813'.6   C2002-904149-X
PR9199.4.R93A73 2002

TRAFFORD

This book was published *on-demand* in cooperation with Trafford Publishing.
On-demand publishing is a unique process and service of making a book available for retail sale to the public taking advantage of on-demand manufacturing and Internet marketing.
On-demand publishing includes promotions, retail sales, manufacturing, order fulfilment, accounting and collecting royalties on behalf of the author.

Suite 6E, 2333 Government St., Victoria, B.C. V8T 4P4, CANADA
Phone   250-383-6864   Toll-free   1-888-232-4444 (Canada & US)
Fax   250-383-6804   E-mail   sales@trafford.com
Web site   www.trafford.com   TRAFFORD PUBLISHING IS A DIVISION OF TRAFFORD HOLDINGS LTD.
Trafford Catalogue #02-0493   www.trafford.com/robots/02-0493.html

10   9   8   7   6   5   4   3   2

Foreword

St. Georges is a fictitious island and its inhabitants have their origin in my imagination. That is not to say that the circumstances described are fictitious or that the sad reality of the Great Divide is not a raw and gaping gash on the body politic of our world. I have tried to give voice to the voiceless and to call forth out of the shadows a handful of souls to share with us their lives and dreams. Though the story is set in the Caribbean and describes the particular circumstances of migrant Haitian workers, similar stories with different protagonists take place all around the globe. We are all made of the same stuff and equally capable of the choices of prejudice, greed, love, generosity and transcendence of spirit. The story is essentially a spiritual love story, a metaphor of hope for us all. The people are very ordinary people, just like you and me. Their lives are a patchwork of everyday trials and tribulations and everyday chances. It was written as a tribute and a witness to the capacity of the human spirit to be transcendent in the midst of the mundane and to illuminate the essential human qualities that bind us all together.

This book is dedicated to the Haitian people working in distant lands, who are a lifeline for the sustenance of many back home and are trading the comfort of their present lives for the future lives of their children.

Nora Ryan

Acknowledgements

Writing this work of fiction was an adventure and a journey of personal discovery. It was a singular act, kept mostly to myself – with the exception of my husband, who gently encouraged me throughout the endeavor without intruding on my need for distance from all that bound me to my other world. Two dear friends, Phito Jean-Pierre and Jean-Pierre Bazile, assisted me with the Creole translations. My deepest thanks for their patience and support during a time when one of them knew little English and the other was on a few rare days of leisure.

An author may write alone but certainly cannot get published without the additional work and encouragement of a team of supporters. My thanks to Lorna Lynch of AI Editing for her work on the first draft and to Pat Verge for her reading and editing assistance at a later stage. Special thanks to Margaret Ardan for her careful reading and editing of the final draft.

O CHILDREN OF MEN!

*Know ye not why We created you all from the same dust?
That no one should exalt himself over the other.
Ponder at all times in your hearts how ye were created....*
- Bahá'u'lláh

ACROSS THE GREAT DIVIDE

Part I

CHAPTER 1

GONAIVES HAITI

Nous ne vivons pas ici — nous existons — nous existons comme les chiens, "We do not live here — we exist — we exist like dogs," observed Josef, more to himself than to the other men as he quietly finished his ten-hour work day. He squatted down to rest, before starting his four-mile cycle ride home.

His lean, muscular body was taut. His ebony skin glistened with the sweat sucked from his pores by the relentless heat and sun that had beaten down on him throughout the day. The beads of moisture had joined to form two rivulets that trickled between his eyes. They slowly followed the outline of his chiseled nose, coming to rest on the up-curve of his lips. He lifted the ends of his T-shirt and wiped his face with slow, deliberate strokes.

Comme les chiens, "Like dogs," he quietly repeated. He thought of his work week — blisters, muscle strain, and a few miserable gourdes. Enough for food, which was plentiful. Never enough to get ahead and rise out of the poverty that seemed to be his lot. His cycle ride home in the dark was filled with anxiety. A meek man who always traveled unarmed, he was prey to the gangs who made their meager living by despoiling others.

Tonight he was lucky and made it home unscathed. He shared the cluster of shanties he called home with an assortment of relatives: his aging mother, a brother and sister-in-law, and their three children. The compound consisted of a jumble of low-slung wooden buildings in a yard fenced with sheets of corrugated iron. He arrived to find the family sitting and chatting around the glowing embers of the charcoal fire on which they had cooked their supper of rice and plantain. They usually ate together outside under the shade of the mango tree that grew in the yard. Josef loved his family, but today his heart was heavy. He barely nodded a greeting as he slipped into his own tiny shanty that held an assortment of worn and tattered books in the small cabinet, his only piece of furniture. He lit his paraffin lamp, and took out a large black-bound Bible, his constant companion for the past five years. Tonight he chose a passage that always salved his weary heart. He sat back on his heels and intoned the verses with fervor.

> *Le Seigneur est mon berger,*
> *Je ne manque de rien.*
> *Sur de frais herbages, Il me fait coucher,*
> *Près des eaux du repos, Il me mene,*
> *Il me ranime....*

> "The Lord is my shepherd,
> I shall not want.
> He maketh me lie down, in green pastures,
> He leadeth me beside the still waters.
> He restoreth...."

A cockroach scurried across the floor and disappeared under his bedroll. The distraction was enough for him to reflexively lurch forward and slam the bedroll with the palm of his hand, dropping the Bible in the process. He slowly lifted the cotton batting to check his accuracy and found the flattened remains of the cockroach on the dirt floor, its smeared innards impressed on the cotton batting. Josef grinned, picked up the Bible, reverently kissed its outer cover, and put it back in the cabinet. He carefully moved the cabinet to one side and lifted the reed mat on which it had stood. Underneath was a coffee jar, sunk in the dirt. He lifted it out and counted the contents – twenty five hundred Haitian dollars, about five hundred U.S. dollars. After five years of scrimping and saving, he finally had enough to get illegal passage to the States. Tomorrow he would get a *tap-tap* to Cape Haitien and catch the next boat taking illegal immigrants to the U.S.

~ ~ ~

Josef sat at mid-ship, crammed between two large, powerful-looking males and three young women that looked to be in their twenties. Smooth-skinned, high-cheek-boned, good-looking women, with eyes filled with a mixture of fear, hope and resilience. One of them looked pregnant. Down in the hold were twenty other souls who had desperately committed their life savings to the captain. A fellow Haitian, he traded in dreams that had slim chance of being realized. The forty-foot sloop lumbered through the sea. Its clinker-built hull, aged and barely sea-worthy, creaked and groaned with the strain of its human cargo. Josef had brought enough food and water for four days, but the winds had been unfavorable and the seas high. They were now more than six days at sea. Josef was feeling nauseous and thirsty. He was well used to hunger, but the combination of sea spray and constant rocking was starting to make him feel disoriented. Suddenly he heard the triumphant cheer of one of the passengers.

"La terre, Miami!"

A wave of expectation moved through the passengers and many who had retreated down into the hold came out to witness their deliverance. They watched and cheered as a group of low-lying islands came into focus. But the cheers of exultation were quickly quenched by the captain, who had spotted a marine patrol boat about three miles off starboard. He ordered everyone who could fit into the hold to retreat out of sight and continued his course towards the islands. The deep blue shortly gave way to the aquamarine of shallower waters and approaching reefs.

The overloaded sailing sloop was no match for the speeding patrol boat. Josef was now crouched behind a large coil of ropes and tarpaulin on the bow of the boat. As the patrol boat came closer, the letters *H.M.S. Caroline* came into focus. The captain swung the rudder hard to the leeward side in an attempt to change course and prevent the patrol boat from getting into a position where it could inspect the sloop more closely, but the combination of the wind and the ship's uneven load caused it to broach. The sea poured over the listing vessel and into the hold, engulfing the terrified occupants. Josef heard the crunching, tearing and ripping of wood on coral as the boat was swept onto the reef. There was panic on the top deck and a sickening silence in the hold. Josef was swept overboard and pulled by the current towards the reef. Others were in the water, swimming towards the patrol boat. The crew were throwing lifelines, but Josef turned from the safety of the patrol vessel and started swimming towards shore, which he judged to be about two miles away.

For an hour he was thrashed about in an unforgiving sea, its only mercy being its buoyancy and warm temperature. As dusk approached, the sea calmed. Josef summoned his energy and will to survive and pushed slowly onward toward the beckoning lights.

Mon Dieu, Mon Dieu, aidez moi, je vous supplie, "My God, My God help me, I implore you," he gasped, each stroke now becoming more weary as his waterlogged body became heavier by the minute. He started to lose all sense of time and place, concentrating his efforts on keeping his limbs moving through the briny liquid that threatened to swallow him whole and suck him down into its depths. Finally, the sea heaved him onto a sandy beach. Josef stopped struggling and cried silently, his face pressed deep into the warm dry sand. He rolled over on his back, prayed and gave thanks. He slowly picked himself up and started to walk towards the lights. The silhouette of a man came into sight. As he came within earshot, Josef called out to him.

"Miami?" He pointed towards the lights.

"No," came the reply, "You on St. Georges, man."

CHAPTER 2

CANADA

"I hope you're ready for this, Elizabeth Bourke," she said aloud to herself as she folded the letter. It was the sixth time she had read it.

Dear Mrs. Bourke:
The Ministry of Education for the Eastern Islands is pleased to offer you a teaching position. (She could recite each phrase by heart if necessary) *We anticipate your arrival on September 6th 1996.* (The day after tomorrow) *The terms of your contract are ...*
(Barely enough to get by on in Canada)
Two years ago she would have been really excited. Now she was not so sure.

She looked at herself in the mirror. Was that tired-looking forty–year–old face really hers? Those slow and brooding hazel eyes? She sighed, turned and looked out the window, surveying the empty pasture. The wild prairie grass was now coarse and stringy as it took on its autumn hues of brown and ochre. The clumped patches of uneaten vegetation were telltale signs of its former inhabitants: well-fed horses, who avoided manure-tainted forage. There was clarity in the air, suggestive of early snow. Images of snowdrifts and sagging fence wire flashed through her mind's eye. She shifted her attention to the yard.

It was bare and free of clutter. The auction had made a clean sweep of the assembled pieces of garden and stable equipment that she and Matt had accumulated over the years. The once productive garden was now matted with vegetable debris. The raspberry bushes still flourished. They were the only evidence of the hours of laughter, work, squabbling, and love the two of them had shared. She twisted her plain gold wedding band and removed it, twirling it between her fingers with reverence and love.

"I wish you were coming, Matt," she said softly. She went into the living room and curled up on a well-worn sectional, the one remaining piece of furniture. She looked around the bare room. The blank walls stared back at her. Smudges and marks recorded the minor altercations that had occurred over the years. The space felt hollow and empty. Not much living being done in this room anymore. A flood of emotion engulfed her. She cried. Loud and cathartic at first, then quietly, wet, salty tears washing down her cheeks. The flash flood had overcome her practiced defenses, had overflowed and eroded through scar tissue. She was not yet healed. When it finally subsided, she lay limp and lifeless, a spent salmon after spawning. She fell asleep.

He came to her in her sleep. Slipped in beside her. They nestled together in an S, gently jostled with each other as they had done for the past twenty years. Then they lay together motionless like a well-fitting glove. She was awakened by the ringing of the phone. He had already left. She was on her own again. It was the estate agent. All the papers had been signed; the sale was final. She would come and collect the keys later that afternoon.

~ ~ ~

At the airport, she had clung to her daughter while she issued a string of advice.

Finally, Michelle had broken from her mother's clasp. "Mom, I'm almost nineteen. I'm a lazy bum, but I'll survive. I've got it all figured out. I'm going to live on subs all week and make a heaping great pot of spaghetti and sauce at the weekends. Then, when I come and visit you at Christmas, you can indulge me with all my favorite dishes – deal?"

"Deal."

Now the small twin-engine airplane swooped low over a sea of aquamarine and deep blue, startlingly clear and visible. As they approached St. Georges, Elizabeth spotted a wrecked wooden sailing sloop. She wondered how long the ancient vessel had been perched on the reef.

CHAPTER 3
ST. GEORGES

"Do you like the house, Mrs. Bourke? We just done painting it," beamed the broad-framed man, as he handed Elizabeth the key. "I hope you enjoy your stay in St. Georges, Ma'am. If you got problems, just call three four four five nine and ask for Charlie."

Elizabeth surveyed the small, neat two-bedroom house, with its white walls and corrugated green roof. It was furnished simply. It didn't compare very favorably with some of the other houses she had looked at, but the rent was very reasonable and it had a large fenced-in yard.

"It looks just fine, Charlie. I have a great view up here on the ridge," she replied. "I can see the sea from both sides. What about water, is it included in the rent?"

"No, Ma'am, but you got a big tank and all de gutters work. You should be okay for water. We got plenty of rain last month. De tank, she full. If she runs low in de summer, call public works. Dey bring a load from water plant."

"Thanks, Charlie, bye for now." She waved him off as he rattled away in a beat-up black truck.

~ ~ ~

There were three suitcases and one large crate to unpack. Elizabeth sat on the rattan sofa, picturing where she would place everything. The two framed prints of the Canadian landscape would look nice on the freshly painted living room wall. Two picture frame brackets were conveniently in place already. She would put the bookshelves on either side of the arched alcove, which separated the dining from the living area. The computer could go into the spare bedroom. It was going to look cluttered, but that was nothing new. And all those books and journals she just couldn't seem to let go of – they had followed her down to the Caribbean. She would just have to find room for them. But where? The large collection of "National Geographic" was in the first of the boxes marked 'books' that she unpacked. They may be of some use to the kids at school, or she could always donate them to the library.

She had spent the first week in a small hotel by the beach, having arrived two weeks before school was to reopen after the summer. She had had time for a leisurely introduction to life on the island. The town was a settlement on the western low-lying part of the island; it spread from the center on either side and meandered its way into a series of small distinct groupings. Beach Street was the tourist strip, with its pleasant restaurants, Bermudan-style post office, and government buildings. Mostly wooden facades, with shaded verandas. Some of the older homes were bolstered up with beams, salvaged from the mighty log masts of ships that had foundered on the jagged reefs that ringed the islands. Full of charm and color, the street finally petered out into a jumble of shanties locally referred to as Little Haiti.

Elizabeth had been shocked and intimidated at first when her walk had brought her through this settlement. She did not know how to react to the expressionless faces that watched her as she made her solitary journey through the quarter. The buildings were shabby and poorly constructed, with outhouses that looked particularly precarious. Some had a splash of recent color, while others were sun-faded to a gray-brown. She chanced a smile and greeting with one woman who was washing clothes in a large tin basin. Her overture was returned with a broad smile and eyes that suddenly became animated. This encouraged her. She became braver in her approach, and tried out her high school French on two men sitting on a wall. They were passing pieces of paper between them and speaking in hurried, hushed tones.

"Bonjour."

" Bonjour, Hello," replied the taller of the two.

Vous avez de travail pour moi? "Have you work for me?" asked the small guy, as he quickly stuffed the pieces of paper into his pocket and pushed himself off the wall to approach her.

"Non, pardon."

"Touriste," speculated the tall one and he started to speak in a French that Elizabeth could not understand. The little guy backed away smiling and held up his hand in a gesture of deference. She smiled and continued her walk.

As she wound her way out of this settlement and down onto the street that ran parallel to it, she encountered small groups of well-dressed men and women on their way home from church. Many of them held their Bibles over the sides of their faces as sunshades.

The sun was piercing its way to earth through a defenseless blue and cloudless sky. The remnants of old salinas, once used in the salt raking industry, dominated the landscape in a patchwork of large flat ponds. Egrets and herons stalked their shallows, and small fish could be seen swimming in the canals that led from the ponds to the sea. A pungent odor was coming from the salina that day, marring its attractiveness.

As she made her way back to the hotel, a young man selling conch shells, his hair in the Rasta style of dreadlocks, stopped Elizabeth. He was barefoot, and his eyes had a glazed and far-away look. Elizabeth bought a shell, the first of many she would collect over the next few months. She reached her hotel room feeling hot and sticky. She quickly changed, headed down to the beach, and plunged headlong into the turquoise water. The sea was cool enough to refresh, yet warm enough to luxuriate in. She basked in it for over an hour.

Elizabeth spent several hours in the local library, trying to pad out her scanty knowledge of the history and socio-political makeup of the islands. There was very little available literature devoted to the Eastern Islands as an entity, other than a few glossy pamphlets unabashedly aimed at the tourist market. Most of what she unearthed were footnotes and afterthoughts in volumes describing the Caribbean as a region. All former slave colonies, their checkered history revolved around their relative importance as either an economic or strategic military location for one or other foreign power.

The Eastern Islands' one claim to fame was their former importance as salt-producing islands, supplying salt as far afield as the cod fisheries in Newfoundland. The salt industry had foundered and finally ground to a halt in the sixties. It was now being replaced with the golden calf of tourism, and while this tourism had taken off on some of the other islands, St. Georges appeared to be largely in genteel decay. Its position as administrative capital of the islands allowed it an air of self-satisfaction, while it waited for the *manna* that was generally expected to be ready to descend on the island at anytime.

Elizabeth visited the grocery stores and shops, trying to get an idea as to what was available. She quickly realized that stock in the grocery stores was dependent on weekly shipments of supplies from Miami. Those with purchasing power would quickly swoop in and empty the shelves of fresh produce, leaving them conspicuously bare, displaying only dried goods for the rest of the week.

It was on one of these excursions that she had met Grace.

"Hi, there, you look new," Grace chirped, her broad drawl revealing her American background. "My name is Grace Richmond. My husband works with one of the investment companies here. What brings you here?"

Elizabeth looked at the flamboyant American, dressed in floral cotton shorts and matching blouse. She looked in her early fifties, was slightly overweight, and her pale skin suggested that she either never went outside, or that she plastered herself in sunscreen at all times.

"I'm Elizabeth Bourke. I'm here on contract with the Education Department. I will be working with primary school children, in a catch-up program. Nice to meet you, Grace."

"Where are you staying? Nosy, ain't I?" Grace chortled.

"I'm staying at the Beachside Resort this week, but I'm looking at moving to a house up on the ridge next week."

"Great! We're going to be neighbors," Grace squealed. "Oh, by the way, don't buy your meat here. It's better at Francine's down on Middle Street," she whispered, cocking her head to the freezer load of unrecognizable meat cuts. "Got to fly, hope to see you again real soon." She disappeared out the door.

Elizabeth smiled to herself. *Well, she's a character. A bit of a steam roller perhaps, but definitely friendly.* She had met a number of the expat community that week, most of them there on contract from the U.K. as part of Britain's human resource aid to its Dependent Territories. The resident white population was, for the most part, a revolving door of these professionals, many of whom had made a career in the foreign service and had numerous previous postings to other former colonies. Elizabeth, being a Canadian and under the direct employment of the local government, found herself in a different category. Without the ready-made network of support, she would have to reach out across the boundaries to form friendships. This suited her just fine, but she suspected that it wasn't going to be easy.

~ ~ ~

Elizabeth sat amidst a heap of packing paper, sipping coffee. The burst of energy with which she had first attacked the task had dissipated. Though all the large pieces had found homes, she was still faced with a ridiculous amount of bric-a-brac and unsorted books.

"Yoo hoo! Anybody at home?" came the unmistakable drawl.

"Grace! Come in, your timing is perfect. I'm just having a cup of coffee. Care to join me?"

"You got the coffee, I got the cookies." She breezed in with a tin full of freshly baked walnut chocolate chip cookies. "Well, this looks like fun." She plunked herself down on the nearest chair, placing the cookies on top of a box marked 'duvet'. "Don't think you'll need that here," she said, "unless we get a whole week of a miserable sixteen degrees like we got last December."

Elizabeth looked at her new friend. "I suppose not," she said with a wry smile. "That duvet was a wedding gift. It's been through a lot. I need it for emotional warmth, if nothing else."

"Your husband not with you?"

"He died, just over a year ago."

"Sorry," Grace whispered and became silent.

She then eyed the stacks of books and started to casually sort through them. "You like to read, I can tell. I'm very perceptive," she said, self-mockingly. "You're not a religious nut, are you?" she asked as she selected out copies of the *Bible*, the *Koran*, and the *Bhagavad-Gita*. "And what's this?" she asked, pointing to a book titled *Bahá'u'lláh and the New Era*.

"I don't think I'm a religious nut, but loosing my husband put me in a tail-spin that I'm just starting to crawl out of. I'm still trying to make sense of it all. My childhood faith, Catholicism, somehow does not fill that hollow. So, for now, you could call me a seeker. And that particular book was given to me by a friend who is a Bahá'í. The Bahá'ís basically believe in the unity of religions and the unity of humanity. What about you, Grace?"

"Bob and I are both Methodists, but I wouldn't consider myself particularly religious. I try to be a good Christian. To be honest, I don't think about it much really. A seeker? Hmm… tell you what I'm seeking right now, is another one of those cookies!" They both laughed and left the subject.

"You've got a big yard, you'll probably need help with it," Grace said. "Get yourself a Haitian gardener – they're the best, they're very hard workers. They do all the laboring jobs on the island."

"We'll see. The yard looks pretty tidy right now, I may be able to keep on top of it myself."

"Why bother – you're going to be working pretty hard. It won't cost a lot to hire a Haitian. By the way, I'm having an afternoon tea, on Thursday. Come along and you'll get a chance to meet some of the other ladies."

"Thanks, Grace, I'd love to. I'll be starting school the following Monday, so it will be my last chance to hang out for a while."

~ ~ ~

The schoolyard was bustling with children, all laughing, jostling, and shouting to each other as they made their way to class. The girls wore orange gingham pinafores over white blouses, and the boys wore khaki shorts and short-sleeved shirts. They watched with interest as the white lady made her way to the principal's office.

"I hear she take over from Miss Jones," one boy said. "Jason, Terry, come here!" he shouted. "The new grade five teacher is a white lady!"

The school consisted of a number of neat wooden buildings

with glassless windows, some of which had their storm shutters closed. There was a smell of fish and frying coming from one building, and through the open door, Elizabeth could see a stout aproned woman attending to a number of pots.

Elizabeth entered the principal's office and introduced herself to Mrs. Clark.

"Welcome to Cecil Jones Primary School, Mrs. Bourke," Mrs. Clark said.

She was a chubby, heavily bosomed woman, with fat, dimpled cheeks and spectacles. Her hair was gelled back into a tidy bun. "You will spend the morning with me. I will introduce you to each class. But first, let me show you the resource room. It will be your office."

As the two women made their way through the yard, they were followed by groups of children eager to see the newcomer.

Mrs. Clark fingered through her keys until she found the right one. "Here it is," she said with satisfaction. "I will have a key made for you next week, Mrs. Bourke."

She opened the resource room door.

There were six small desks and one large one. The walls were lined with a series of simple shelves, displaying a variety of readers of all levels.

A sudden loud clanging rang through the mayhem in the schoolyard, followed by the clatter of over two hundred pairs of feet as they skipped, jumped, and thumped their way along the wooden veranda to their classrooms. There was a brief silence, followed by a chorus of well-timed voices, which Elizabeth judged to coincide with the reciting of the daily prayer.

As the two women made their way back to the principal's office, Elizabeth noted the different sounds emanating from each classroom. Some were quiet except for the commanding voice of the teacher. Others suggested a tentative balance between students and teachers. A few produced such a cacophony of sound that Mrs. Clark rattled her keys on the offending doors, issuing warnings of retribution. "Let's give them fifteen minutes to settle down before we take our tour," she suggested with a smile.

~ ~ ~

Josef had spent the first month drifting between the anonymity of Little Haiti during the day and the shelter of the bush at night. Terrified at the thought of being caught and sent back to Haiti, he had cowered under the vicious thorns of a large acacia bush, often soaked to the skin and desolate. Immigration officials had been making swoops on the shanty town at night in search of Haitians without work permits. It was believed some of the Haitians who had been on the sloop may have managed to swim ashore. Many had drowned. The rest had been rescued, given forty-eight hours to recover from dehydration and shock, then promptly returned to Haiti. St. Georges had absorbed thousands of Haitians onto its shores over the years, and sympathy for a disaster such as this was short-lived.

Gradually, the night raids became less frequent, Josef's terror subsided, and he started to sleep in a small shanty that was occupied by another Haitian. Sylvio, a wily veteran of two years of illegal residency, had taken him under his wing, told him where he might safely look for work and where to avoid. He had brought him to the north shore to fish for shark. They had gone out on Sylvio's homemade skiff and dove for conch together. Some of Sylvio's dealings didn't sit well with Josef. He was into a numbers racket. Gambling was definitely something that Josef disapproved of, despite its widespread and legal existence in Haiti.

But, tonight, even Josef felt lucky. More than that, he felt blessed. Not only had he found work two days that week, but he had gone to church for the first time. He had sung and prayed. Had felt a warmth and a spiritual calm take over his body and soul. He was starting to feel human again. He, Josef Jean Claude, could read and write, and speak French fluently. He was a skilled mason. Surely it was only a matter of time before he would find someone who would help him get a work permit.

He started to sing as he made his way down to the sea. He

followed the donkey track that led to a quiet tract of beach, out of sight of the nearest road. He undressed down to his underwear and waded into the shallows with a bar of soap. He began to wash away not only the dust and grime, but also a portion of the indignities he had suffered over the past several weeks. He sat in the shallows and quickly washed his boxer shorts. He replaced them with haste, modesty preventing him from remaining naked any longer than he absolutely had to. Then he enjoyed the luxury of relaxing. Immersing himself in the sea, he slowly turned on to his back and allowed the quiet surf to gently raise and lower his outstretched body in a rhythmic, lilting tango between sea and man. And he dreamed of a future, which was free of fear and full of opportunity. Yes, perhaps he would still get to Miami.

Later, he emerged from the tide and combed the beach for any useful discards that had been belched up on shore. He found a slightly broken but serviceable plastic crate, two intact glass bottles, and the prize find of a glass fisherman's float. It must have been in the sea for many years and may have traveled in the currents from as far away as Portugal. This he could definitely sell to either a tourist or one of the resident "blancs" who seemed to like that sort of thing. *Grace à Bon Dieu*, "Thanks be to God," he exclaimed as he placed his treasures in the crate and made his way back to where he had left his clothes. He shook them out well, dressed himself, and headed back down the donkey path, considerably richer than when he had started out.

Sak Pase? "What's happening?" Sylvio greeted him in Creole as he entered their shared quarters. The two men huddled over the booty and decided how to best utilize each item. The bottles could be boiled clean and used as water jugs. The crate had multiple uses, as a chair, a table, a storage area. And the glass float! That should fetch twenty dollars.

Bon travay! "Good work!" exclaimed Sylvio and he gave Josef a congratulatory slap on the back.

The next day, Josef decided to take a walk up the ridge and check out the houses there for work. Sylvio had told him that for yard work, most people didn't ask questions. There were some big houses up there with lots of trees, which meant lots of leaves to sweep up.

CHAPTER 4

From: Bourke@caribsurf.com
To: Michelle@man.ed.com
Date: Saturday, September 28, 1996

Dear Michelle:
                Finally I got my e-mail hooked up. This will be a short message, just to make sure we are connecting. I don't want to spend half an hour writing to you, just to have it gobbled up in cyberspace. So e-mail back ASAP and let me know if we're surfing. The mail is hit and miss and the phones astronomically expensive, so we are going to have to rely on e-mail for most of our communications. I'm fine, have completed three weeks at school. I have a nice house on what is known as "the ridge," with a good view and lots of cooling breezes. By the way the temperature hasn't gone below 23 degrees since I arrived. Any snow yet?
Love Mom.

From: Michelle@man.ed.com
To: Bourke@caribsurf.com
Date: Sunday, September 28, 1996

Hi Mom - got your message! Yes we're surfing!
Have signed up for biochemistry, physics, environmental biology and philosophy. (The philosophy is for laughs, plus it's supposed to be an easy A) Most of my lecturers are pretty OK, but I may be having a bit of a personality clash with the physics lab tutor. He thinks he's Albert Einstein, but he's just a dork with a couple of years' jump on the rest of us. I met Jane from River High last week. We're planning to go to her cabin with a couple of friends next weekend, which means I have to do chores every night this week to make up for being away at the weekend. Jimmy is in fine form. We were jumping four feet high courses last weekend. Hope I can afford to keep him over the winter. I'd like to take him to the Spring Show

this year. Gotta go! I have a lab assignment to write up for dorkman before tomorrow.
Luv Michelle (on second thoughts, I take that back - it snowed yesterday - I hate you)

From: Bourke@caribsurf.com
To: Michelle@man.ed.com
Date: Friday, October 3, 1996

Dear Michelle:
            Glad this e-mail is working and that everything is going well for you. School is fine. The kids are great. They really try hard, but some of them have really gotten off to a bad start and seem to have fallen between the cracks. Kids whose first language is Creole seem to be particularly at risk. The Haitians here work really hard and don't get a lot of respect. But then life is hard for lots of people. I'm amazed at how some people survive. The cost of living is really high. Oh, by the way there are lots of horses and donkeys here – well, tough little ponies, actually. The snorkeling is great here, amazing fish and living coral.
Can't wait to take you out on the reef at Christmas.
Love Mom

~ ~ ~

Elizabeth sat in the yard sipping iced tea, trying to decide whether to continue with the clean-up she had started in the yard earlier that morning, or just sit there until the thought went away. The recent dry spell had scorched and shriveled many of the leaves on the orange cordia and yellow elder trees that shaded the yard. They had hung brittle and burnt until two days of high winds had plucked off the dead leaves, providing a well needed manicure to the trees. The debris was now scattered all over the yard. The hibiscus bushes that had looked so attractive with their deep crimson flowers when she arrived, were now a jaded puce, their dehydrated petals curled tightly together in a deathly embrace. There were two garbage bags of leaves and weeds lying by the gatepost for collection, but there was lots more to be done.

She got up and went to inspect the water tank. It was down a few inches but still had lots of water. Good, but I hope it rains again soon, she thought. She went back to her deck chair, determined to loll about for the rest of the afternoon.

She had drifted into that twilight zone between sleep and wakefulness when she was startled by a knocking on her front door. "Blast!" she muttered, as she went scurrying through the back door. She found some clothes to cover up her swimsuit before attending to the intrusion. There had been no warning sound of a car driving over the cattle grid into the yard. Whoever it was, was on foot.

She opened the front door to be greeted by a clear but heavily accented, "Hello, how are you doing?"

"I'm fine," she answered cautiously as she eyed the medium-framed, wiry looking man who was smiling at her with a frank and open expression. His skin was a deeper black than many of the islanders' and his features were finer. He must be Haitian, she thought. He wore a loose-fitting pair of cotton khakis and a black sleeveless tank top. He was holding something by his side which was covered and wrapped in a plastic bag. On his feet were a well-worn, poorly-fitting pair of sneakers.

"I like to clean your yard. You got one job for me?"

Elizabeth eyed the disarray in her yard. Remembering how hot, sweaty, and exhausted she had been after two hour's work that morning, she decided to give him a go. "Okay, come with me and I'll show you what you can do."

He now looked at her quizzically, clearly not having understood what she had said. She tried again, throwing in whatever she could offer in French. "Venez avec moi," she ventured as she beckoned him to come with her.

"Vous parlez Français!" he exclaimed and his face lit up. He then proceeded to rattle on in French as he followed her to the shed.

Now Elizabeth looked baffled. *Un petit peu, et parlez plus lentement,* "A little, and speak more slowly," she entreated.

Using a combination of mime, English, and French she

showed him what implements she had and what she would like him to do with them. He opened the plastic bag and took out a menacing looking machete, making sweeping motions with it to indicate its uses. He followed her around the yard as she pointed out the tasks that needed to be done.

"Vous comprennez?" she asked.

"Oui, Oui, Je comprend – I hunderstand," he confirmed with evident pleasure.

"Oka-ay." She nodded her head in amusement and left him to get on with it.

She went inside and started to make bread. She didn't really care for the locally made bread, which was invariably white and sweet. Besides, she couldn't lie out in the yard while he slaved away in the afternoon heat.

By the time she had three whole-wheat loaves rising on the kitchen counter, he had collected three bags of leaves and debris. He was now busy using his machete with the deftness of a sculptor, as he cleared tangled vegetation from around the hibiscus and bougainvillea. She watched him through the kitchen shutters bending to his task and singing softly as he worked. The back of his neck was covered in a film of sweat and his tank top had wet streaks running in lines down his curved back. She filled a large glass with iced tea and brought it out to him. He looked at her, at the clean glass, at his dirty hands, and then back at her again.

"It's okay," she said, and offered it to him with an outstretched hand.

He accepted it in his cupped hands and slowly brought it to his lips trying to figure out how to avoid soiling the glass. Tilting his head back, he drank it down in one long series of pleasure-filled gulps and gave her back the glass with the same care with which he had accepted it.

"Merci." He belched slightly. "Je m'excuse," he added.

"You're welcome," she said with a smile.

By the time the loaves came out of the oven, the yard was transformed. Elizabeth was very pleased with the work. She brought a bucket of water, soap, and a towel outside for him to wash up with.

"What's your name?" she asked when he was finished.

"I am Josef."

"Good job, Josef, *un bon effort*," she remarked. She asked him if twenty dollars was okay, basing the offer on the five-dollar hourly rate that she had been quoted by Grace.

He agreed and she handed him a twenty-dollar bill and one of the loaves in a brown paper bag.

Peut-être vous retournez à deux ou trois semaines? "Perhaps you can come back in a few weeks?" Elizabeth suggested.

"D'accord," he agreed, and turned to start the long walk back down the ridge.

Elizabeth watched as he disappeared down the lane. She wondered if he was a legal or illegal immigrant.

~~~

"My advice to you," Grace said, the next day at a coffee morning hosted by one of the expats, "is not to ask. It's easier to ask forgiveness than permission. Lots of Islanders here give work to illegal Haitians. It saves them money and as long as it's a job that the Islanders don't want, nobody seems to get too upset."

"But have you seen some of the huts they live in?" Elizabeth asked.

"Don't be imposing your values on them," interjected Veronica, a veteran of many overseas postings. "It might not be what either you or I would like, but they're perfectly happy. You should see some of the shacks I've been in, where they actually have a Haitian maid to look after an older person or the children. 'Course they pay them peanuts," she added.

"Have you enjoyed your time here, Veronica?" Elizabeth asked.

"Oh, we've had a pretty good time. We've done lots of sailing, and the people for the most part are very nice and friendly. Don't exactly like to kill themselves working, but we take things as we find them and that seems to have kept us sane over a number of postings."

"As for me," Grace offered, "I'm one of the many spouses who hasn't been able to work while their husband or wife – usually husband – has been here. It's a lot harder for us, which is why we do such ridiculous things as collect shells and bottles, play bridge and chase a golf ball around for half the day."

"Excuse me," Mary pitched in with feigned indignity, "bridge – ridiculous? Would you care to retract that comment?"

"Well, you know I'm no good at card games," Grace laughed.

"Cards! Bridge isn't a game of cards, it's a serious challenge of the intellect, filled with a combination of strategy, bluff and subterfuge."

"That's what I said, I can't play poker either!"

"I think it's time to go," Veronica suggested, "before these two come to blows."

"Oh my goodness! Look at the time," Grace shrieked. "If I don't get home before Arthur, he'll think I've got nothing better to do than to yack with you lot all day."

~ ~ ~

From: Michelle@man.ed.com
To: Bourke@caribsurf.com
Monday, October 6, 1996

Hi Mom:

Had a great weekend at the cabin. We went for a long hike up to Ochre Creek. I tried out my new boots. They're great. We could see lots of elk droppings and could hear them bugling into the night. Jane had to get up to go to the biffy early in the morning and when she looked out the window, she could see a great big bull with six females grazing in the meadow. She woke us all up. We tried to take some shots, but without the telephoto lens, they probably won't be that great. Guess what, I got the only A on my lab assignment. Even Albert Einstein seemed impressed. Sally invited me over for

supper last Thursday and was asking for you. She says she wrote to you snail mail and included her e-mail address. Don't work too hard. Only 50 something more shopping days before Christmas. See you soon.
Luv Michelle

~~~

From: Bourke@caribsurf.com
To :Newera@mantel.com
Date: Sunday,October 12, 1996

Dear Sally:
    Thanks for the card, complete with your e-mail address. I am settling in well, but finding life quite a challenge. There just seems to be so many contrasts for such a small place. The expat community here is really friendly and has been very good to me, but they tend to stick to themselves a lot. The whole society seems to be layered, with little socializing between groups. A lot of diversity, but not much of the "unity in diversity," that you are always talking about. The Haitians are definitely at the bottom of the heap. You wouldn't believe the ancient looking boats they sail over here to trade on. Some of them also bring in illegal immigrants. There was a tragic accident about six weeks ago, when a Haitian sloop carrying illegal immigrants was wrecked off one of the reefs, with many lives being lost.

    The trading sloops arrive about once every two weeks, bringing mangos, grapefruit and lots of charcoal. The charcoal is sold, by and large, to the Haitian population, who mostly don't have electricity and cook over charcoal fires. The boats stay here until everything is sold and then return with a load of everything including the kitchen sink. Last night I went for a bike ride down by the dock and saw them swinging a truck on board. It seemed so incongruous, modern technology being carried across the high seas on a primitive and ancient looking sloop, with wind as its only power. Apparently they are wonderful sailors and tough as nails.

    Work is going well. I love the children, but wish I had a

few more resources to work with. Do you think you could use your influence with Manitoba Education to see if you could round up some fairly recent children's stories, and any resources using phonics would also be helpful. Thanks for inviting Michelle to supper last week. I think her sub diet is starting to wear thin. Come visit me sometime,
Love Elizabeth

    Elizabeth logged off the Internet and shut the computer down, one step at a time as Matt had drilled into her when they first went into cyberspace three years ago.
    "Well, Matt," she thought out loud, "what do you think of the techno-peasant now!"
    She stared out the window over the darkened horizon, broken only by the distant lights of the town. The town was lit up in clusters. The less well-to-do areas boasted only intermittent bursts of illumination, and Little Haiti had disappeared into the oblivion of the night. It was quiet up on the ridge at night. There was nothing to compete with her thoughts and they flooded in on her in great waves. The past presented itself in rose-tinted hues dressed in reassuring cotton prints, while the future stood naked and unadorned like some giant test tube baby waiting to be programmed.
    She undressed wearily and rolled carelessly into bed, wrapping the sheets around her naked body, a barrier between her and eternity. She willed him into her presence, and chided him for not having visited her for over a week. What was it like out there? He wouldn't say, but he took her hand and silently they walked down to the beach together and slipped into the moon-lit water. She brought him to the reef and to the under-water world beneath. They surfaced for breath in unison like a pair of dolphins. Then they were a pair of dolphins, now much stronger than before, diving deep, deeper still. He was leading and she followed. As the last ray of moonlight was absorbed into the darkness, he too was absorbed into the blackness beyond.

CHAPTER 5

The building was filled to capacity. All doors and windows were flung open in a welcoming gesture to passersby. Rhythmic incantations, followed by an ardent chorus of lilting songs, wafted out into the evening air and were carried by the night breezes into the heart of Little Haiti. Josef swayed with his brothers and sisters, singing praise to God in true tones that quivered as they curled around the peaks of the spiritual, before descending, then spiraling up once again into the lofty heights. Tonight he was at a Baptist gathering, one of the three Haitian congregations that he frequented. It mattered little to him which group he worshipped with, as long as he could sing, pray, and read *Paroles de Dieu* (The word of God) or as most of his friends put it *Pawol Bon Dye*.

His French served him well. It gave him a much wider access not only to scripture, but to other books as well. He thought of Fr. Bernard, who had encouraged him all through school. He had given Josef extra tuition to make up for the weeks he missed during the many jobs he worked at from the time he was twelve. Fr. Bernard had hoped that he might become a priest some day. But one night when Josef was sixteen, the Tontons Macoutes, ruthless enforcers of the Duvalier regime, had arrested Fr. Bernard for preaching subversion to the state. The school had been closed the very next day, and that was the last Josef had seen of Fr. Bernard. It was the end of his formal education.

Shortly after that, he had started his long apprenticeship with a construction company in Port au Prince. For five years, he traded his youth for the hope of better wages and a better life, once he was qualified. The hours had been long, the pay little more than his meals during working hours. He apprenticed during a construction boom, but by the time he was qualified, it seems the Americans had lost faith in the iron fist of Duvalierism and were packing up and leaving. For a while it looked like Aristide would bring with him an era of justice and democracy, but that had been short lived.

Josef belonged to that small minority of educated peasants, whose learning had brought insights, but no solutions to their dilemma. Such people felt the sting of injustice and oppression most keenly. But he was not a politician. He abhorred violence and had borne his serfdom with patience and dignity, placing his trust only in God. He kept to himself and slowly gathered his gourdes, one at a time, until he had enough to flee his homeland.

Now the crowd filed out of the building. Many of the young men and women took the opportunity to visit with each other. Some made plans for clandestine meetings. A van was parked on the opposite side of the street about fifty yards from the doorway. Inside were a man and woman. Their blue T-shirts had the word "immigration" written on the back and front, in bold yellow lettering. They counted the bodies as they came out.

"Fifty-seven," said the women, "that's ten more than last month."

"See any new faces in the crowd?" asked the man. "A few new women here for sure.... And look, there's that old rogue, Sylvio, still giving us the slip. And who's that with him?"

"He's getting careless. Time to pay him a visit," said the woman.

~ ~ ~

Sylvio shuffled the cards and dealt out five hands.

Mwen pa ladan, "Don't count me in," Josef commented.

Si ou vle, Francois, ba mwen ron-m lan. "As you wish. Francois, pass the rum to me." The four men sat down on the floor, passed around the rum, and settled into the game.

Josef, lumie-a pi pne-m, mwen pa oue anyin, "Josef, bring the lamp closer to me, I can't see a thing," demanded Emile.

Sylvio ap li kapab fe kokin. "Sylvio is going to swindle us."

Map lis, "I'm reading," objected Josef, but he passed it to them anyway, put away his book and went outside.

It was a beautifully clear night, with plenty of breeze to keep the insects at bay. Josef decided to head down to the beach and try sleeping in a shady location there. Not much point going home; those guys would be at it all night. He found himself a comfortable spot under a casuarina tree and sat down. It had been three months since he had been washed ashore and he considered his progress to date. He no longer feared for his life as he often had in Haiti. But he was without a work permit. The fear of deportation lurked at the edge of his consciousness, ready to leap to the foreground at a moment's notice.

Work was sporadic, and he had to be very careful not to indulge himself when he had a good week or he was left with nothing during the bad weeks. The contractors were in a position to get a work permit for him, but they had enough laborers at this time. He had gotten one painting job, which had kept him busy for three weeks. Then the employer had kept deferring payment. Josef had returned on three separate occasions for his payment, which never materialized. He had reduced his fee several times and had even suggested installments, but all he got in return were excuses and vague promises. Finally, he had left the man to God and had quietly gone on to his next "petit job," rebuilding someone's wall.

He had three yards that he attended to every two weeks. His favorite was the one on the ridge. There, he was treated with respect, and when he was finished the lady would sit down and have a cup of coffee with him. He loved coffee. For him it was luxury, and she served it just the way he liked it, with milk but no sugar. They would try and talk together, but her French was funny. She would bring her French dictionary out to look for words she didn't know, and when she spoke in the present but meant the past she would say, "le passé," or if she meant the future, would say, "le futur." She was nice. He liked her.

A Haitian sloop had arrived today, and tomorrow he would go down and help them unload. They always gave him a basket of fruit for his help. He would bring her some mango when he went to clean the yard on Saturday.

At five in the morning Josef was awakened by the rivalry of the island's many roosters. The early morning din was added to by the barking of dogs and the intermittent braying of donkeys. Josef gave thanks for the new day, checked his surroundings, stripped to his shorts, and went for a swim. He combed the beach while he was drying off and found a large tangled hank of fishing net. Confident that he would find a good use for it, he picked it up and brought it back to where his clothes were. He put on his clothes and returned home. As he approached his shanty he noticed a small crowd gathered outside.

Sak Pase? "What's happening?" he inquired cautiously.

Li te pran, Sylvio, Francois et Emile, "They have taken Sylvio, Francois, and Emile," they replied.

~ ~ ~

Elizabeth looked at the two children quietly working away on a simple exercise she had given them. They were brother and sister. Marie was nine and in grade three; Gustaf was eleven and in grade five. Marie looked small for her age, with delicate features and huge brown eyes that clamped onto Elizabeth like a magnet, sucking every piece of intelligible information from her teacher. For all Marie's keenness, she was quiet as a mouse and spoke so softly that Elizabeth had to lean close to her to catch what she was saying. Gustaf had the same high cheekbones and thin nose as his sister. His features, however, were chiseled out in rougher contours, on a more sturdy frame. He was more ebullient and he fired out incorrect responses with the same eagerness as correct ones, a feature that was a source of great frustration to his classroom teacher. Elizabeth had decided to work with them together as she had hoped that they could help each other out at home. But they had not made the progress that her initial assessment had indicated. She decided she should try and speak with the parents.

"I finished, Mrs. Bourke," piped up Gustaf. She walked over to examine the work. All the questions had been tackled, in a sprawling script and truncated phrases, phonetically spelt.

"How are you doing, Marie?" Elizabeth asked after correcting Gustaf's work. Marie silently pushed her copy towards her and raised her eyes, attaching them to Elizabeth's as securely as a hat on a hook. Marie's work was neat but only partially completed.

"Read this question for me please, Marie," she said,

encouraging Marie to discover and correct her own mistakes. Marie nodded and took her eraser to make the necessary changes.

"Well done, Marie. Now, do you think you can finish the rest at home?"

She nodded.

"Well, that's enough for the two of you for one day, I will see you next week. It's okay for you to help her, Gustaf," she added.

He puffed with importance as he gathered his things to leave. "Come, Marie, let's go. I help you. Bye, Mrs. Bourke."

Elizabeth made her way to Mrs. Clark's office to try and catch her before she left. The office was cluttered with boxes and books. Mrs. Clark emerged from under a large pile of notes and office accounts.

"All this has just come in," she said with a chuckle. "I wanted this four weeks ago, you know. Now I have to deal with it at Christmas time." She paused briefly and then asked Elizabeth how she could help.

"I'm worried about Gustaf and Marie. They are both bright children, but their reading has not improved as much as I would have expected. I'd like to talk to their parents."

"That's going to be difficult. I've never met the father and their mother speaks very little English. Know any Creole?" she asked. Elizabeth smiled and shook her head. "I haven't seen the mother at all this term," Mrs. Clark continued. "She used to sometimes walk home with them after school. I wonder if something is up?"

"Mrs. Clark, if you could please get word to the mother to be here at eight thirty on Monday morning, I'll work on finding an interpreter."

"This is a real problem for us, Mrs. Bourke. Our school has more Haitian children attending than any of the others. We have been looking for extra help in teaching English as a second language. We had a Haitian man teaching for a while using a special government grant. But when the money ran out, no one was prepared to pay him to continue. We had to let him go. He had a family to support and couldn't work for nothing. By the way, do you have any ideas for the Christmas

29

concert? It's coming up in three weeks."

"I'll put my thinking cap on over the weekend. What date will the concert be held on?"

"December twenty first."

"Great! Michelle will be here in time to see it. Have a nice weekend, Mrs. Clark."

"You too, Mrs. Bourke."

Elizabeth tidied her desk and locked the resource room door. She walked across the empty schoolyard to her bicycle, and swung her bag over her head and shoulder to secure it during the trek home. As she mounted the bicycle, her skirt parted to reveal the culottes she was wearing. All the teachers dressed formally for school, especially the females. Elizabeth had endless trouble reconciling her mode of transport with the dress code, and after trial and error had decided that smart culottes were her best option.

As she wound her way home, she greeted many nodding acquaintances. Some of them sat on walls, or tooted in recognition as they passed in their cars. Her favorite exchanges came with fellow cyclists. She would pass them each morning as she whizzed by on her way down the ridge. They were bent over their bicycle frames as they heaved themselves up the hill to tend gardens or build houses. Many would look up as she passed and greet her with an "Okay, Okay." On the way home they were in full throttle and passed her with a wave and an expansive smile. There were others who walked this route daily, mostly women who cleaned house, did laundry, and sometimes looked after babies. She had not hired anyone to clean the house for her. The tiled floors maintained their sheen with just a quick sweep each day to pick up the inevitable dust that found its way in through every crack and under every screen door. She often washed the floors and cleaned the bathroom on days when Josef was working in the yard. He had been coming regularly now for the past three months, and just recently she had asked him to come each Saturday, instead of just every second week. This way he could help her with some work around the house. In fact tomorrow might be a good time to do the windows. They had a coating of salt and dust that had been building up for months. She wanted the place to look nice for Michelle. She had ordered a nice light-weight cotton spread for the spare room, with a matching lamp shade. She hoped it would arrive in time.

~ ~ ~

There had been lots of rain over the preceding week and already the hibiscus was blooming again. The orange cordia were dense with new foliage and a few blossoms were starting to peak through the greenery. Josef was washing the outsides of the windows, while Elizabeth tackled the insides. She was about two windows ahead of him, her technique consisting of a quick squirt with washing fluid followed by a furious rub and buff with the cloth. He, on the other hand, used water and wiped the windows dry with slow deliberate strokes, until he was satisfied with the results. He hummed quietly to himself until she interrupted him.

Chantez! Chantez! "Sing! Sing!"

He raised his voice and sang with delight. By the time they had finished it was almost six o'clock.

"Stay for supper, Josef? Maybe you can help me," she inquired.

He looked at her inquiringly, not quite understanding, but he nodded.

"Okay, Madam, I stay." He went to the tap by the kitchen door, turned the water on and liberally squirted the liquid soap she had given him onto his cupped hand and over his dark skin, splashing the water over his shaved head. He took his worn and faded T-shirt off to splash and cool his torso down.

"Here," Elizabeth interrupted. "See if this fits." She handed him a large T-shirt she had been given to mark Education Week, but had not yet worn. She then retreated inside, resurfacing dressed in a simple cotton print skirt and blouse. He was sitting outside on a deck chair waiting for her.

"Come in, Josef." She beckoned him into the kitchen. She handed him the bag of mangos he had brought, and asked him to peel and prepare two of them. She took some potato salad from the fridge and quickly made a tuna salad to go with it.

The meat in the stores looked so unappetizing in unmarked frozen slabs that she had all but given up on it. She had been eating a lot of beans and peas. Tonight she had some leftover peas and rice, an island staple that had become part of her culinary repertoire. She put them in the microwave.

"Some fresh homemade bread and I think we're in business," she said. "Please sit, Josef." He hesitated as he made his way to her table, but she smiled and indicated a chair for him. "Please."

"Would you like to say grace, Josef," she asked on an impulse.

"Yes," he agreed. He bowed his head and in French that was too eloquent for her to follow, he gave thanks for both of them.

"God bless you," he said to her across the table when he was finished his prayer, "And God bless me," he added with a grin.

They ate the meal as though they were conducting a language class. She added words to his English vocabulary; he corrected her French and threw in the odd word in Creole for amusement.

"Josef, I need your help," she said at last. Then she tried her best to explain in broken French and with the assistance of a dictionary, that she needed an interpreter to help her talk to the mother of Gustaf and Marie.

"No problem, I help you, Madam." Then he corrected himself: "I will help you."

"Thank you. Coffee, Josef?"

"Yes, it's good for me," he replied.

"How are you doing here, Josef? Is it okay for you?" she asked.

He shook his head and turned the corners of his smile down into a frown. "It no good for Haitians here. I no got work permit. If I found, I go back to Haiti." Then he broke into rapid French and told her how his friends had been picked up by immigration, and that he had to move from where he was staying as it was no longer safe for him there.

"*Plus lentement, plus lentement.* Slower, slower, Josef," she requested and they muddled their way through.

"Can you help me?" he said at last.

"I will try, Josef, *mais je pense qu'il sera très difficile*, but I think that it will be very difficult."

"I go now," he said. *"Merci beaucoup."*

"Monday at eight thirty?" she asked.

"D'accord." He turned and walked off into the darkness.

She went inside, poured herself the last of the coffee, curled up on the sofa and watched TV.

He took a winding stretch of sand-surfaced road. It brought him to a deserted and dilapidated beach house he had scouted out earlier that day. He had swept the glass and debris from one room and had neatly arranged his worldly possessions — a bed roll, a multipurpose crate, a bag carefully stuffed with clothes, a box of books, and an oil lamp. He lit the lamp and opened his book. Reading required his full concentration, but the satisfaction he got from it made the effort well worth his while.

~ ~ ~

Elizabeth was shocked by what she saw. The woman facing her looked gaunt and weary. Her skin, a dull charcoal, was stretched like parchment over her protruding cheekbones. A faded stone-washed blue dress hung limply over her emaciated body. She looked around the room with languid eyes. Yet she sat poised and had returned Elizabeth's greeting with a fleeting smile. When Josef spoke, her face lit up and her expression changed to one of hope. Her eyes focused in on him, like a moth drawn towards a candle. Elizabeth had no idea what he had just said to her, but whatever it was, it had definitely opened the door for communication. Elizabeth took out the list of questions, which she had painstakingly translated into French the previous evening. She needed to know if Gustaf and Marie had a place to study at night, if they had a routine that encouraged them to read the books she had lent them, if they were getting enough sleep, if they were getting enough to eat.

The answers went something like this:

Yes, as long as there was light and it didn't rain. They

studied outside on a bench.

Yes, when she was feeling well she told them stories in Creole and then had them practice their reading, but she had not been well for some time now. Sometimes they got enough sleep and sometimes they got enough to eat. If friends came by with food, they stayed late but the children were well fed. When no one came around, they had time to sleep but not enough food. She worked whenever she could. On those days Marie and Gustaf made supper, which took a long time over a charcoal fire. There was not much time for study afterwards.

Elizabeth now departed from her notes. "Where is your husband?"

"My husband is dead, Madam."

"Do you have family here that can help you?"

"I have no one, except a cousin and an old aunt."

"You have two lovely intelligent children," Elizabeth told her. "You should be very proud of them."

"Thank you, Madam."

Elizabeth was at a loss for anything else to say. She knew she had been talking to a dying woman. Josef continued his own conversation with the woman for a few minutes before bringing the meeting to a close. Elizabeth watched the woman respond with appreciation to the warmth in Josef's voice.

"I will try and find someone to bring you home," Elizabeth offered.

"That's okay," Josef responded, "She lives close. I walk with her."

~~~

"That woman looks really ill," Elizabeth said to Mrs. Clark.

"Yes, I've seen this before. AIDS," she said in a lowered voice. "I wonder how long she'll last."

"What will become of the children?"

"Well that depends on whether she has relatives who can take them in or not. Quite a few of these children end up in foster care. People are afraid of AIDS here; she may well be almost totally deserted before the end."

Elizabeth sat at her desk staring vacantly out the window. A familiar sickness started to leak back into an area in her being that had just started to feel pleasure again. Memories of Matt's last weeks started to flood in. The long night vigils and the semi-conscious days, where pain scraped away at one's innards and anguish ravaged the soul. Finally, a reconciliation with fate was achieved; they walked through the valley of darkness together, holding a flickering candle of faith that became more illumed as they penetrated further into the abyss. But this was no journey for children to make, and she felt a surge of maternal protectiveness towards the two children who were being pushed towards the precipice. She reached inside her desk and took out the little brown prayer book Sally had given her.

Thy name is my healing, O my God, and remembrance of Thee is my remedy.
Nearness to Thee is my hope, and love for Thee is my companion.
Thy mercy to me is my healing and my succor in both this world and the world to come.
Thou, verily, art the All-Bountiful, the All-Knowing, the All-Wise.

Words intoned in desperation. Quiet calm. A silence within. She waited for an answer.

~ ~ ~

From: Bourke@caribsurf.com
To: Newera@mantel.com
Date: Monday, November 30, 1996

Dear Sally:

Thanks for the books you sent. I think they are going to be a big help. I'm afraid I've come to you cap in hand again. What resources might we be able to beg, borrow or steal regarding English as a second language? There are a lot of Haitian nationals here who would really benefit from English lessons. I'm thinking about starting some night classes for parents. This might help both parents and children integrate into society here. Many of the children are falling behind in their schoolwork because of a poor grasp of English and their parents are unable to assist them. Add that to the huge social and economic challenges they face, the greatest of which is a searing prejudice towards them, and it's a wonder they survive at all. I'm afraid I'm not in the best of humors right now. I think I just came face-to-face with my first AIDS victim, the mother of two of my pupils. I couldn't even converse with her properly because of the language barrier. I felt completely inept. If it wasn't for the help of Josef, my gardener, the meeting would have been a complete disaster. What's that you were saying about the need for a universal auxiliary language? Count me in!

On a brighter note, Michelle arrives in two weeks time. I'm so excited.

I think she will really like it here. It's a fabulous place to come for a holiday. It's the living that gets tough. Having her here will force me to lighten up a bit.

My love to you and Ken,

Elizabeth

CHAPTER 6

"Hi, Mom, over here," she waved.

"Michelle! You're early!"

"I was the only one scheduled on the three o'clock flight, so the pilot decided to leave ten minutes early. He let me sit in the cockpit with him. It was really neat."

She gave her daughter a long, enthusiastic, swaying hug.

"It's a wonder you didn't walk across the water from Flamingo Island," Grace piped in. "If your mother is anything to go by, you're just about capable of it. Hi, I'm Grace, your cab driver and guide for today."

"Hi, Grace, I've heard about you."

"Where are your bags Michelle?"

"I just brought my rucksack," she said, hitching it up on her shoulder. "Here, take this, Mom, it's from Sally," she said, as she thrust a bulging carrier bag to her mother.

"Okay, we're off then." The three women got into the idling jeep, parked conveniently just outside the entrance.

"Do you want to take the freeway or the scenic route?" Grace joked.

"Let's take the scenic route," decided Michelle.

"Good choice! Only choice, but good choice," Grace said.

They rattled their way out of the car park and over the cattle grid, a vital piece of landscaping to keep donkeys and horses off the runway. Elizabeth watched her daughter as she enthusiastically absorbed the sights, sounds, and smells that assailed them on their way home: passengers in the backs of pickup trucks; school children slowly making their way home after a stop at the ice cream store; dogs barking; cars honking good naturedly to their friends; a row of men picking up litter along the side of the salina, HMP printed on the backs of their T-shirts.

"What does HMP stand for? And what's that smell?" Michelle asked crinkling up her nose.

"Her Majesty's Prison, and the smell is the salina," Elizabeth replied.

"On a good day!" Grace added.

They wheeled up the road towards the ridge and Elizabeth

hung out the side of the jeep, exchanging waves and greetings with the bicycle brigade.

"How do you know all these people?" Grace asked.

"We see each other every morning going to and from work. Look, Michelle," exclaimed Elizabeth as the road leveled out on top of the ridge. "Sea on both sides."

Michelle looked to the east, over the steep ridge, down at the long strip of white sand, licked by a mirror-calm azure sea. Then to the west, across the long gently-sloping, bush-covered, sweep of hillside, which flattened out to merge with a long narrow inlet of the sea. "Wow! It's amazing."

Grace maneuvered the jeep over and around the bumps and pot-holes that marked Elizabeth's driveway and came to a jolting stop at the front porch.

"Home sweet home." Grace announced.

"Thanks, Grace, coming in for coffee?"

"Thanks, but I think I'll just leave the two of you alone together, this evening. Don't worry, you'll see lots of me, Michelle."

"Nice meeting you, Grace. See you soon," Michelle said.

"Well, what do you think?" Elizabeth asked. She escorted Michelle through the front porch, past the alcove that separated the dining area from the kitchen, and down the narrow hall into her bedroom.

"It's great, Mom. Nice bedspread."

"I'm glad you approve. Bathroom is just across the hall. Go easy on the water, okay?" Michelle flopped on the bed, unloading her rucksack with an enthusiastic jerk onto the floor. She rolled over and peered out the window. "I don't believe it, cacti growing in the yard. I guess I'm not dreaming, I'm really here." She turned around, curling her well-shaped slim legs into a V as she sat on the bed and smiled at her mother.

"Guess what's for supper." Elizabeth said.

"Lasagna?"

"That's right."

"Great, I'm starving."

"Let's go eat then. It's ready."

~~~

"I'm so glad you're here, I've really missed you," Elizabeth said as she raised her glass to Michelle.

"Me too."

"You've got three weeks here, and for two of those I'm on holidays, so we should be able to do lots. Maybe even some island hopping."

"Well, I'm pretty easy, but one thing is essential: I have to go back with a tan. There is absolutely no point in flying down to the Caribbean from the frozen north, if you don't go back with a tan."

"I'm sure that can be arranged, but be careful and use lots of sunscreen. The sun is really vicious here, especially in the middle of the day." Elizabeth noted Michelle's pale complexion, dotted with a few winter-weary freckles. It won't take long for those to multiply and come to life, she thought, remembering how freckled she was by the end of a Canadian summer.

Michelle ran her fingers through her sandy hair. It was cropped short and gelled to spike up cheekily at irregular angles. Her boyish good looks went with her athletic approach to life and no-frills style of dress. Yet, it was clear from the softening in her body contours that she had matured into a very attractive young woman.

"Tomorrow I've school in the morning, but have the afternoon off. How would you like to cycle in with me? You can coast around and have a look at the place, maybe visit the museum, and we can go snorkeling later on in the afternoon?"

"Sure."

~~~

Next day, they set off at seven thirty in the morning, Elizabeth's usual time. After the exhilarating trip down the ridge, their pace slowed as they wended their way down Middle Street and then through a warren of back alleys. Elizabeth had discovered them through trial and error, in an attempt to find the shortest route from Ridge Road to the school. A small crowd was gathered outside a long, and narrow, low-roofed building. Most of the people were carrying buckets.

"That's the water distribution plant," Elizabeth said. "Half of the homes don't have running water or sewage. Those who can afford it have a good gutter system to collect rainwater in large tanks and have their own septic system in place. The smaller houses collect some runoff from their roofs, but come here for drinking water."

Further on, Elizabeth pointed out the bakeshop. A faded sign marked "Fresh Baked Bread" barely identified the spot.

"However did you find that place?" Michelle asked.

"By accident," Elizabeth returned.

As they rounded into the schoolyard, hoards of smiling faces greeted them.

"Morning, Mrs. Bourke. Is that your daughter?"

"Good morning, Jason. Yes, this is my daughter."

Michelle gave them all a cheery wave, said goodbye to her mother, and headed off for a morning of exploration.

Out of the corner of her eye, Elizabeth spotted Marie and Gustaf quietly making their way to their classrooms. Marie walked close to her brother, her intelligent eyes tentative and unassured.

Elizabeth parked her bicycle and walked over to them. "Good morning, Gustaf and Marie, how is your mother?"

"Today she fine, but last week she really sick. Aunt Jessie stay with us all last week, but today she go home," Gustaf replied, his eleven-year-old face burdened beyond its years. Marie looked up into Elizabeth's face, her eyes brimming with tears. Elizabeth took her hand and gently led her to her classroom.

She then made her way back to Mrs. Clark's office. "I've an idea for the Christmas concert," she said.

"Good, what is it?"

"Well, we have a lot of Haitian children here, many whose parents don't understand English very well. I thought it might be really nice for those parents to hear one song in Creole."

"I'm not sure what the other parents will think."

Elizabeth persisted. "I have six students, four of them Haitian, who come to me at the same time for reading. Two of those are Gustaf and Marie. Something tells me that this may be the last Christmas concert their mother may ever attend. Let's make it special for them."

"Well, okay," Mrs. Clark agreed. "Who are the other two children?"

"Michael Bean and Tunisha Lightbourne."

"Let's just stick with the four Haitian children this time around and see how it is received."

"Thanks, Mrs. Clark."

~ ~ ~

"So, how was your morning, Michelle?"

"Very interesting. I checked out the museum and the library. Everybody knows you there."

"Yes, well that's because I bring groups of students there," Elizabeth said.

"I also stopped by the dive shop to check out the price of taking a resort dive course. Ninety bucks. What do you think?"

"This was going to be a surprise, but I've already booked you in for a scuba diving course. You may never get this kind of opportunity again."

"Gosh, thanks, Mom! Sure you can afford it?"

"Ah, what the heck. But don't expect too many phone calls from me in the new year, strictly e-mail. Come on, let's head to the beach while the visibility is still really good."

Michelle led the way, as if she had lived there all her life.

"Take the next left," Elizabeth shouted from behind. But Michelle had already passed the turnoff and Elizabeth had to pedal hard to catch her. "Wait, you've gone the wrong way," Elizabeth barked, and Michelle finally stopped.

"I can see the beach from here," Michelle argued. "Can't we just keep going?"

"Okay, we'll give it a try, but these roads can be very misleading."

True to her misgivings, the road took a sudden turn to the right and ended abruptly in a dead end of three huddled shanties. Elizabeth was just about to wheel around, when she heard a voice.

"Mrs. Bourke, Mrs. Bourke!" It was Marie.

"Marie, so this is where you live."

Marie came up to her and took her by the hand. "Come."

The women parked their bikes and followed Marie as she led them between two of the shanties and out into the back. There were two large shady orange cordia trees with a hammock made from a patchwork of fishing net strung between two of the branches. Sitting on the remnants of an old arm chair, looking wan but content, was their mother. Seated on a wooden bench directly under the hammock, huddled over a book, were Gustaf and Josef.

"Josef?"

"Hello, Madam," he said with a warm smile and he stood up to greet her.

"So, you're the person who has been helping them with their reading."

"No, they teach me," he said with a laugh.

"Well, it's working," she said. "They have both improved considerably in the past few weeks."

"Considerably?" asked Josef. "What is that vocabulaire?"

"An pil," Elizabeth explained drolly, using a Creole expression. "This is my daughter, Michelle," she continued. Smiles, handshakes all round.

"Ask your mother, Gustaf, if she is coming to the Christmas concert."

"She says, 'God willing', ma'am."

"Good, because you two are going to sing a special song to her in Creole," she whispered to Gustaf. His face lit up. "I'll tell you all about it at school tomorrow, okay?"

"Okay."

"Bye now," she said as she turned to go.

Josef walked with them back to their bikes. "See you on Saturday, Madam."

"See you, Josef," she confirmed.

"They couldn't all possibly live in that little hut, could they?" Michelle asked as they slowly cycled away.

"Well, they cook outside. They study outside. And judging from the hammock in the trees, at least one of them sleeps outside."

"What did he mean, 'see you on Saturday'?"
"He helps me around the yard."
"Their father works for you?"
"He's not their father. It's a long story, I'll tell you about it later on this evening. Let's go snorkeling."

~~~

The sea was calm and inviting. Elizabeth pointed to an area where the waves were breaking, about two yards from shore. "If we swim out to that reef, we'll see loads of living coral and plenty of fish."

They put on their fins and adjusted their masks, spitting into the corners and rubbing the fluid over the glass.

"This really is disgusting, Mom. Are you sure this is the way to keep them from fogging up?"

"Trust me, just rinse them lightly when you're finished, it really helps."

They started to swim out, faces towards the bottom, scanning the crystal clear shallows. A small shoal of blue tangs came into view, shimmering mauve in the bright sunlight. Following closely was a magnificent queen triggerfish, its electric blue smile lines spreading from its nose to its gills, highlighting its turquoise and yellow body with benevolent grace.

Michelle came up, breathless. "Did you see that!"

"Yes. Just wait until you get to the reef. Then you'll really be impressed."

They swam on and soon reached the first stretch of reef, submerged under only about five feet of water. The coral was abundant: huge globular mounds of brain coral with tiny damsel fish swimming between the grooves; elkhorn and finger coral were everywhere and the snap and crunch of parrot fish could be heard all around as they grazed on the algae-covered coral, turning rock and coral into fine sand as it passed through their bodies.

Elizabeth pointed to the swaying stands of yellow and purple sea fans. Butterfly fish, rock beauties and angelfish all graced the scene. They hovered on the surface, captivated by the spectacle. The sea kept them afloat as they lay suspended, on the shimmering surface, which formed another kingdom, another world.

As they leisurely swam back to the shore, Elizabeth wondered at how the sea world was separated from the land world by a transparent liquid, yet was veiled from everyday sight. She thought about the layers of life that coexisted on land, separated by an even thinner physical layer, but just as unknown and unheeded by the casual traveler. Her thoughts went back to the shanties, to the families they sheltered, and the hopes and aspirations that emerged from their cramped quarters. Their lives were so different, and yet she knew their hearts felt the same pain, joy, and yearnings that were felt by the hearts on the ridge.

They reached the shore and took off their fins, snorkels, and masks, placing them in the carrier bag Elizabeth had left on the beach. Towels on the sand, they stretched out and soaked in the late afternoon rays, warm and embracing, no longer searing.

"Fifteen minutes only," Elizabeth cautioned. "That will be enough for one day."

She closed her eyes and surrendered herself to the simple pleasure of an ocean-cooled body being reheated by the rays of a now tempered sun. After ten minutes on one side, she turned herself as she would a pancake, golden on one side, ready for its final browning. She looked at her watch and gave herself an extra five minutes.

"Right, time to go," she said on the stroke of four, "before you turn into a lobster."

They climbed the ridge slowly, in silent contemplation of their shared experience.

CHAPTER 7

He had been quietly tending the yard for two hours. They had scarcely spoken and he had been working to his own plan, carefully choosing which shrubs to trim and which to leave alone. She was making bread and was completely preoccupied in her thoughts. The scene at the shanty was constantly preying on her mind. A doomed woman living on the edge. Two children with an uncertain future. And this man, who two months ago was nameless and formless, was forcing her to reconsider the very order of her existence. Not that she hadn't thought of the circumstances that cause great divides between people, be it poverty, class, creed, ignorance, or race. But it was always from the comfort of the abstract, from an educated middle-class position. This somehow shielded one from guilt, spared one from immersion in its visceral depths. But a small island can goad one into confrontation, where one must choose to look or turn away. Elizabeth had dared to look. It had made her uncomfortable. Why had he asked her to help him in this way? Wasn't it enough that she had given him work? What possessed her to think she might actually be able to help? She punched down the dough, and fought with its sticky glutinous hold as she divided it between the three pans, putting them aside for the final rising.

He tapped lightly on the kitchen window. *Je suis finis.* "I'm finished."

She opened the door, her hands still gooey with dough.

C'est tout? "Is that everything?" he asked.

"C'est tout," she responded. She didn't invite him in.

"You okay?" he asked.

"I'm okay, Josef. It's just that, *je suis très occupé aujourd'hui,* I'm very busy today," and she showed him her hands by way of explanation.

"I hunderstand," he said and he smiled.

She paid him and he left.

Five minutes later Michelle came bouncing into the kitchen. Her hair was wet and her eyes slightly reddened from prolonged immersion in chlorine treated water. "Well, I had my first pool session. It went well. There's quite a bit of equipment to get used to, and the oxygen tanks are heavy. It took me a while to get used to breathing through my regulator, but I got the hang of it." She gave her mother a hug. "I met Josef on the way down. He seems really nice."

"Hmm, hmm," Elizabeth replied absently. "I've made an early supper. Grace has invited a few people over for drinks afterwards. You're invited."

"Is it okay if I pass, Mom? I'm kinda tired."

"I'm kind of tired myself, but I'd better make an appearance at least," said Elizabeth. "Grace has been very helpful in introducing me to the expat community here. They seem like a nice friendly bunch, and it can be pretty isolated here for someone on their own."

~ ~ ~

"Going to the Governor's Christmas party on the twentieth?" Mary asked. She spoke with an upper crust English accent, and carried her large angular frame with grace.

"I got an invite. Do you think it would be okay to bring Michelle with me?"

"Yes, visiting family are always included in these invitations. It's the social event of the year. You absolutely have to come."

"The police band will be playing," Arthur said. He was squat, rotund and two inches shorter than his wife, Grace. "Have you ever sung *Silent Night* to a Calypso beat before?"

"All the ministers will be there with their wives," Veronica added.

"It's a collection of who's who on the island. Everybody dressed in their glad rags, us included," Grace said.

The conversation diverted to government ineptitude, and all had a go at the system. It was generally agreed amongst those who had spent time in other foreign service postings that St. George's was as tough a place as any.

"What's it like at your school, Elizabeth?" somebody asked.

"I have the kids who are struggling, so it's hard for me to judge. If they had more teachers and a lower student to teacher ratio, it would help. It's especially hard for the Haitian children whose first language is Creole."

"Oh, for goodness sakes, they breed like rabbits," Veronica cut in. "They're going to overrun the country if they don't put a stop to immigration here."

"It seems to me," Arthur said, "that they provide a much-needed part of the country's workforce."

"Is there a minimum wage here?" Elizabeth asked.

"Technically, yes," Arthur said. "But it's so low as to make no difference, and when it comes to illegals working, well there is no minimum wage. It might seem unfair," he added, "but lots of businesses rely on the cheap labor to stay alive."

"If they don't like it, they can always go home," Veronica stated.

"Snacks on the table, folks," Grace chirped, her timing impeccable as always. Ooohs and aaahs went all round.

"You're amazing, Grace," Mary commented, accentuating the pun. "What I don't understand is how you can put such delicacies together from what's available on the island."

"I'm a hoarder. If I see anything that I might possibly use in the foreseeable future, I buy it. You never know when it's going to be in stock again."

The conversation bounced back and forth between fishing, tennis and getting off the island for breathers. Politics safely returned to the taboo shelf.

Elizabeth felt weary and made her excuses to leave. She walked the short distance from Grace's house to hers with a flashlight to guide her. She felt like she was suffocating and unbuttoned the top three buttons of her blouse, allowing the cool night air to billow through the cotton, and wrap her in a soothing embrace. She sat for a while on the patio, her unfocused eyes drifting over the blackness in numbed acquiescence to her darkened mood. Michelle was already in bed asleep. She opened the carrier bag full of goodies from Sally. Tapes and workbooks on English as a second language. More books for children of all reading levels. A small, separately wrapped parcel held three small books, one in English, one in French and one in Creole. The English one was entitled *The Hidden Words of Bahá'u'lláh*. A little note attached read, "You may find these will help you keep things in perspective. Love Sally."

Elizabeth opened it and read the first verse.

> *O Son of Spirit*
> *My first counsel is this: Possess a pure, kindly and radiant heart,*
> *that thine may be a sovereignty ancient, imperishable and everlasting.*

And suddenly she remembered a long forgotten line from the Sermon on the Mount: "Blessed are the pure in heart for they shall see God."

~ ~ ~

"Michelle, you have to wear a dress, it's expected."

"Okay," she relented. "But you're lucky I even brought one." Five minutes later she reappeared, looking chic in a short, burgundy satin classic with a mandarin collar.

"You look great!"

"I feel like a geek." Then she added, "Are you sure I look okay?"

"You look terrific. I'll have to beat the young men back with a stick."

"Do you know if there are actually going to be any young men there?"

"No, but let's go check it out, shall we? What about me? How do I look?" Elizabeth imitated a catwalk model.

"Who cares how you look? – just kidding. Actually you look pretty good, Mom, we may both have to carry sticks!" Just then there was a loud honking noise in the yard.

"Our chauffeur has arrived, Madam. Let's boogie."

~~~

There was a line of elegant couples slowly making their way through the greeting line.

"Welcome to Government House, Mrs. Bourke."

"Thank you, Your Excellency. This is my daughter,

Michelle, who is visiting me over Christmas."

"Delighted to meet you, Michelle. Hope you have a nice holiday here."

Michelle smiled and nodded self-consciously, and they made their way into the milling crowd.

The reception was out in the courtyard, which was paved with large flagstones from the local quarry, and was enclosed by a combination of trellis and wall. Large flowering hibiscus partially blocked the wall. Bougainvillea climbed the trellis, and spread its red profusion in a wild showy embrace. A group of uniformed policemen were playing Christmas strains with a Calypso beat, just as Arthur had promised. They were mounted on a wooden platform in the middle of the courtyard.

The atmosphere was upbeat, and the guests formed little chattering clusters as uniformed waitresses made their way from group to group offering smoked salmon, shrimp, and conch fritters.

Elizabeth scanned the crowd for familiar faces. "Look, there's Mary, and she has her daughter with her for Christmas. Let's go over to them."

Mary greeted them and said, "Michelle, this is Jenny. She's here for two weeks. Hope the two of you will be able to spend some time together."

The two young women slipped into easy conversation together, and Elizabeth went up to the bar for a drink. On her way back she spotted Mrs. Clark and went to join her. She was in a teacher cluster. Elizabeth noticed that the clusters were mini-representatives of the society at large: each group sticking pretty much to themselves and, for the most part, color coded. There were exceptions, of course, and Elizabeth's own circumstance had provided her with a bit more flexibility.

"Come here, Michelle. I want you to meet Mrs. Clark, my principal."

As Michelle made her way over to them, she made brief eye contact with a young man who had been watching her for some time.

"Michelle, I've heard a lot about you. Nice to meet you. Are you coming to the school concert tomorrow?" Mrs. Clark smiled.

"Yes, I'm looking forward to it."

"Excuse me, how are you doing, Mrs. Clark," came a polite interruption.

"Stanley! How are you? I haven't seen you in ages. What have you been up to?"

"I've been away at school, but am home for the holidays. I'm working at the dive shop over Christmas. How did you enjoy your first lesson?" he asked, directing his question to Michelle.

"I really enjoyed it," she smiled.

"Do you two know each other? Elizabeth asked.

"We haven't been formally introduced. Hi, I'm Stanley Robinson." They all chatted for a while until etiquette demanded that they circulate. Elizabeth studied the young man who was obviously intent on her daughter. He had the typical good looks of many of the young men of the island, not knock-down-dead looks, but pleasing and comfortable. His skin tone was even blacker than most and he held himself with assurance. Later on, Elizabeth would learn that he was the son of one of the ministers.

"Nice seeing you again, Mrs. Clark. You always were my favorite teacher," he said, turning to Mrs. Clark and then to Elizabeth. "Bye, Mrs. Bourke." And finally, "See you tomorrow, Michelle."

The gong sounded and the Governor spoke. He welcomed everyone to the Christmas party and announced that it was now time to sing some Christmas songs. Sheet music with words was handed out to everybody. The clusters dissolved into one mass of swaying happy bodies as they belted out the traditional carols. The police band did its community proud, and a few well-known politicians were drafted to give a rendition of *Hark the Herald Angels Sing*.

~~~

"Well, that was more fun than I thought it was going to be," Michelle said when they reached home.

"Yes, it was nice," Elizabeth agreed. "It felt a bit odd singing Christmas carols in plus twenty-five degrees as opposed to minus twenty-five degrees though. Tomorrow night is the school concert, so that will be another slice of island culture for you to experience."

~ ~ ~

The auditorium was filled to capacity. Grandparents, parents, aunts and uncles took up rows of seating space, and toddlers alternatively sat on laps and ran up and down the aisles. There were three doors to the auditorium; all were open and all had a bulging crowd standing in them. Mrs. Clark made her way to the stage amidst the general tumult, and she stood waiting in silent determination for attention. The crowd settled down as toddlers were scooped up and plonked in waiting laps and outstretched arms like dollops of ice cream.

"Honorable Chief Minister, Honorable Minister for Education, parents and well wishers, welcome to Cecil Jones Primary School Christmas Concert," she announced, when the quiet had met her expectations. "The children have worked very hard and have prepared a special evening. I hope you will give them your full attention. Our first item is an opening prayer performed by the kindergarten class."

The kindergarten students were all dressed as angels with little silver, foil-covered cardboard wings. They didn't have halos. They didn't need them. The chorus of aahs that greeted their arrival was enough to assure them that they could do no wrong. Expertly guided by Miss James, who formed every word with her lips but emitted no sound, they were flawless. Thunderous applause rewarded their efforts.

Next was a selection of tunes from the grade six band. This was slow and painful, with intermittent screeching from errant instruments. The audience was assured by Mr. Handfield that the band had made great progress. The musicians were given the benefit of the doubt by an indulgent crowd.

And so the concert proceeded, with musical interludes followed by Christmas poems and stories. The final performance was a Christmas medley from the grades four, five, and six choir. The program read: *Silent Night*, *Whose Child is This*, *Away in a Manger*, *De pu Lontan nan Betleem*, and *We*

Wish You a Merry Christmas.

Elizabeth peered through the crowd, and two rows from the back she found what she was looking for: Mrs. Jean-Pierre, the mother of Gustaf and Marie, flanked on one side by Josef and on the other by a stout lady, whom she judged to be Aunt Jessie. Her hair was neatly braided and she had a smart red dress on, trimmed with a white collar and large white buttons. Her eyes lit up as Marie, Gustaf, Wendy, and François made their way to the front of the choir for their rendition of *De pu Lontan nan Betleem*. The bulging crowd around the doors took particular interest in this selection. Unable to contain their delight, they joined in, for the final chorus. There was evident pride, and the sheer joy was palpable. The majority of the audience was unsure how to react to this sudden turn of events. There was a mixture of laughter, chatter, and polite applause.

Mrs. Clark then walked to the front of the stage and encouraged everyone to stand up, join hands and sing along with the final song, *We Wish You a Merry Christmas*. And they did, hands joining from door to bulging door. Mrs. Clark tipped a wink at Elizabeth, who nodded her head in pleasure.

Marie and Gustaf came to give Elizabeth a hug before they left. She walked with them to their waiting mother. They hugged each in turn: their mother, their aunt and Josef.

"You sang very well, Marie and Gustaf," he said.
Elizabeth greeted each one of them as they extended their hands warmly to her.

"Mèsi, mèsi Madam," Mrs. Jean-Pierre said, her smile and earnest expression conveying the message of gratitude.

"I wish you all a wonderful Christmas together," Elizabeth replied. "See you after Christmas, Marie and Gustaf, and keep up with the reading."

"We will, Mrs. Bourke."

~ ~ ~

Michelle was studying her scuba diving manual. Now on Chapter Three, she was feeling very comfortable with the material.

"So, Mom, if you should accidentally become entangled in an aquatic plant what would you do?"

"Probably panic."

"N-o-oo. You're supposed to stay calm, not struggle, and work slowly to free yourself. You should take a dive course, Mom, I think you'd enjoy it. Is it okay if I go out tonight?"

"It's Christmas Eve, Michelle, where are you going?"

"I won't stay out late. Stanley invited me to get together with some of his friends for a pizza after he gets off work. He's going to pick me up at six, if that's okay."

"Sure, why not," she relented. "I've still got a few report cards to finish writing up."

"I promise I'll be back by ten, and we'll have a game of Scrabble before we go to bed."

"You're on."

Michelle went back to her manual and Elizabeth started to work on her reports. At about quarter to six, Michelle headed for the bedroom and changed into a clean pair of jeans and a tank top. She spent some time on her hair and came out smelling of peach mousse.

At six o'clock on the dot, a black sports Pontiac rolled over the cattle grid and gave a polite hoot at the front door. Elizabeth went to the door with her daughter. The window was rolled down and Stanley flashed a smile at Michelle. He wore dark glasses and had a large gold chain around his neck. "Good evening, Mrs. Bourke," he said politely.

As she watched them disappear down the drive, she started to have some misgivings. She didn't know whether it was the car, the glasses, the gold chain, or the very blackness of it all. She reminded herself that she had no idea who Michelle might be seeing in Canada and counseled herself to chill out.

She went back to her work, but couldn't concentrate. Why not? She scolded herself. You know nothing about this young man. Will they be alone? Can he be trusted? She went to the drawer and took out the Scrabble board and started to set it up with the intention of playing her right hand against her left – a practice she had taken up since coming to the island. As she was flipping over the last of the tiles, there was a knock on the front door. She opened it and was greeted by a spruced up, neatly dressed Josef.

"*Joyeux Noël, Madam.*" He handed her a box wrapped in plain brown paper.

Elizabeth was dumbfounded. She looked into his eyes for an explanation. His face lit up in a disarming smile. She had no option but to accept it for what it was: simply a gift from a warm-hearted man.

"*Merci beaucoup, Josef,*" she said at last. "Please, come in." She brought him into the living room and they sat down by the coffee table where the Scrabble was laid out. "Can I open it now?" she asked.

"Yes, yes," he said eagerly.

She opened it carefully. Inside was a hand-painted coffee pot stand, in the unmistakable bright colors and motifs of Haitian artisans.

"It's beautiful, Josef. How about a cup of coffee?"

"Yes, it's good for me," he said and laughed.

Elizabeth got up and put on the kettle, then prepared a tray with cups, saucers, milk, sugar, and a plate of shortbread she had made. When she returned, Josef was busy examining the Scrabble tiles.

C'est un jeu? "It's a game?" he asked.

"Yes, would you like to play?"

"Yes, but I don't know."

"Okay, here's how we're going to do it," she said. "You get to use this." She handed him the French dictionary. "But, you must make English words. *Les mots anglais, seulement,*" she repeated.

And so they began. They laughed and cheated, rearranging the board as it suited them, trading Scrabble pieces as they saw fit. The game was over in an hour with no accurate score tallied.

"Now," said Josef, "We make French words, *c'est juste.*"

"Okay, but this time, I get the dictionary."

The second game was taken a bit more seriously, until Josef threw the odd Creole word in, which started a good-natured trilingual argument.

Amidst the furore, in walked Grace. "Merry Christmas! I

see you've got company."

"You know Josef, Grace." But Grace had clearly never had much of an impression of Josef, and his present garb had confounded the situation. "He helps me in the yard, remember?"

"Oh, that Josef. I didn't recognize you."

Next on the scene was Michelle, followed closely by Stanley.

"Hi, Grace, Hi Josef," Michelle said nonchalantly. "I see you started the Scrabble without me. What's this? samedi? froid? lettre? And what the heck is priye?"

"Josef is cheating, he's using Creole words as well as French."

Stanley was quickly introduced to Grace and Josef, and asked if he would like a coffee. "Thanks, but I really had better be going," he said.

"What time you have?" Josef asked, looking at his bare wrist.

"It's ten o'clock," Grace answered.

"I must go too," he said.

"Stanley, would you mind giving Josef a ride?" Elizabeth asked.

"No problem."

Elizabeth and Michelle went to the door to see them off.

"Merry Christmas, Josef," Elizabeth said, and she held his outstretched hand warmly between her two.

"I'll phone you," Stanley said and he kissed Michelle on the cheek.

Both women returned to a slightly off-color and befuddled Grace.

"I'd better be going too, I just came round to invite you for a Christmas breakfast of sausage rolls, crepes, and mince pies tomorrow morning," she said.

"We'd love to," Elizabeth said, and she walked out to the car with Grace.

"Have you lost your mind, Elizabeth?" Grace asked in a hushed, urgent tone.

"What do you mean?" Elizabeth asked, a touch defensively.

"What do I mean! You let your daughter out with an islander. Don't you know they have a terrible reputation for womanizing? And – I find you entertaining your Haitian gardener in your living room! Honey, you need a breather!"

CHAPTER 8

Four men on two bicycles pedalled their way down Main Street. The passengers sat on the crossbars, holding the water bottles and lunch bags. It was six in the morning and there was a nice fresh morning breeze. They chatted excitedly in Creole about the new project at the harbor front, a fifty-bed extension to the Ocean View Hotel.

The hotel overlooked a wide sweeping bay of pristine water, ringed with a coral reef, which broke the fury of the waves during even the roughest of winter conditions. The reef provided calm and tranquility to swimmers and reef life. The hotel's proximity to unparalleled snorkeling and diving locations had, in recent years, made it a favorite amongst the more active vacationers. The new extension was intended to cash in on its new-found popularity.

At six in the morning there was not a vacationer in sight. The front courtyard was quiet, except for the swish of the gardener's broom. He began his daily routine by sweeping the leaves, carelessly strewn by a constantly shedding grove of orange cordia.

The men made their way around the back to the south side of the hotel where the extension would be latched on to the existing structure. When they arrived, they found a crew of ten had already reached the site ahead of them. But for once, they were all needed and no one would be sent away disappointed. A large placard marked the site: *Thompson and Company Serving St. Georges for over 20 years.* Thompson was an American contractor with a big name and powerful influence. The men all recognized it and took comfort in its reputation.

The ill-tempered subcontractor, a huge, dark, and hulking man named Robinson, barked impatiently at the gathered men. A grizzled and aging Haitian relayed the instructions in Creole to the assembled men. Masons to the left, carpenters to the right, and laborers stay put. Josef made his way to the left. There were only three others. This was good.

"Work permits?" Robinson growled.

Four carpenters and two masons produced work permits.

He approached the two masons without permits and gave them a menacing look. "No more work permits for construction workers. If immigration turns up, you two are on your own. Until then, don't give me no trouble."

A white jeep with the Thompson decal rolled onto the site. A tall American got out and walked around, examining the clearing job and foundation work the crew had completed. Satisfied, he turned to the subcontractor and his eager, smiling workforce.

"Everything in order?"

"Yes, sir, Mr. Thompson, everything in order."

Thompson had a quick look at the assembled men. They were a bit raw looking for his taste, but he was already overextended on his other two sites.

"Okay then, more building supplies will arrive at ten o'clock. You have enough to get you started." He turned and left.

Robinson reviewed the work plans with his foreman. "Assign some workers to the masons, and they can start on the perimeter wall. The carpenters can start on the scaffolding. Get a couple of those young boys to dig a latrine. I'm going to check on the other site."

Before long the work-site was a raucous hive of activity. The deep grunting voice of Lennox, the foreman, could be heard at regular intervals above the chattering higher tones of the Haitian workers.

"Don't put de shit hole there," he hurled at the two young men, merrily digging a hole. "De pipe go there," he said, referring to the plans. But they looked at him without comprehension. "Dumb Haitians," he muttered, and added a few choice expletives as he led the two men to a new latrine site. Then he went to check on the perimeter work. He nodded at Josef as he inspected his work. It looked okay. Josef had two men helping him and they were starting to get into a rhythm. He smiled to himself as the foreman moved on. He started a quiet lilting song as he mixed his mortar and spread it with unhurried, deliberate intent.

At noon the work came to a standstill. The men were free to leave until two, then return and work until six in the evening. Some went home to their families for the one hot meal a day, which their wives had prepared over charcoal. Josef and his friends stayed and shared their bread and cold salted fish. They would find a shady spot and sleep as soon as they were finished.

As Josef and his companions slept, two tourists passed by on their rented scooters. "No wonder nothing works here, they're all so bloody lazy."

~~~

Within a few days the work-site started to develop its own order. The external scene was still one of high-pitched frenzy followed by periods of relative quiet; but an internal, unspoken order was forming. Natural leaders had begun to emerge, and the crew had started to organize themselves around these leaders, more for reassurance than any deliberate attempt at forming a power base.

Josef's English was improving all the time. His skill and quiet patience had numbered him among the leaders and had brought him to the attention of the foreman. Lennox was crusty and crude from years of thankless labor, but he recognized good work. He could see how the men were grouping around the leaders, and as long as nobody got out of line, it made his job easier. He would sometimes call Josef, Pierre, and Claude together to discuss the day's work after Robinson had left. Robinson came to the site every morning to check the work and issue orders for the day. Everybody was on edge for as long as he was around. He had threatened to fire one of the young laborers, Jacques, on the third day for arriving thirty minutes late.

"Plenty more where he come from," he had grunted, but had relented when the foreman suggested he just dock his pay. "Dock half a day," he said. "That'll teach him not to sleep on my time."

On Friday, the boy was so intimidated by Robinson's presence that he had dropped a block on Josef's foot when he saw his truck arrive. Josef had stifled his pain after an initial howl, knowing that Jacques' job was on the line. By the time he took his sneaker off that evening, his big toe was a swollen red and purple mess. He cleaned and soaked it in salt water, but the next day he had to stuff it back into the same old dirty pair of sneakers. Jacques looked exceedingly contrite as Josef limped into work, and he stayed close by all day, fetching and carrying for him.

Robinson arrived at four o'clock with the payroll. Lennox gave him the list of names, their hours and work classification. They filed up to him one by one, and he handed out the wages in wads of notes stuffed in envelopes. Those with work permits got pay stubs with typed calculations of their entitlements. Those without permits got a wage based on Robinson's own calculation of their worth and expendability. He handed out the wages to the illegals with a twisted grin that dared them to question his numbers. Nobody protested.

Jacques offered Josef his bicycle until his foot was better. Josef accepted, dropped Jacques at his house, and headed up the ridge.

~~~

Michelle was jubilant after her final dive. Elizabeth accompanied her on the boat to the dive site. She took photographs of Michelle entering the water, and snorkeled on the surface while Michelle made her descent. The clarity was excellent, and she was able to follow Michelle's movements at thirty feet. She watched her disappear over the edge of the coral wall and descend to sixty feet into the deep blue chasm.

Michelle was one of four divers led by the head instructor and closely followed by Stanley, a master diver. The dive went well, and Michelle had completed all her skill requirements with proficiency. Elizabeth had taken some underwater photographs of her as she made her way back to the surface. She hoped the cheap, waterproof disposable camera would do justice to the expedition.

"Tonight we celebrate," Stanley whispered in Michelle's ear as he helped her out of the water. "Pick you up at eight."

~~~

They returned to the house, expecting to find Josef working in the garden, but there was no sign of him.

"I'm starving, Mom. Diving really makes me hungry."

"Okay, how about a nice fat salad sandwich on some French bread?"

"Sounds a bit like a sub to me. But okay, I guess I'd better get used to the idea of subs again since tomorrow is my last day."

"Where are you planning to go with Stanley tonight?" Elizabeth asked.

"We may go to the night club, but I'm not sure," she replied, somewhat defensively.

"Michelle, I know tonight is your last night and I don't want to put a damper on your celebration, but please be careful."

"Mom, I'm eighteen, almost nineteen, I can handle this. Don't you trust me?"

"I trust you, but I'm not sure about Stanley. He's just a bit too charming at times."

A hot streak of anger flashed across Michelle's face.

"Give it up, Mom! At least we speak the same language."

"What's that supposed to mean?" Elizabeth retorted as she went to her bedroom to change.

They ate in silence, except for polite requests for water or mayonnaise. Then Michelle excused herself from the table and said she was going for a nap. "Leave the dishes, Mom. I'll do them when I get up."

Elizabeth went outside to water the plants, leaving the dishes as requested. The hot peppers looked healthy. Small and firm, just starting to turn red. She had tried one the previous evening in a chili and the results had been spectacular: a kick in the taste buds that sent Elizabeth and Michelle diving in unison for the water jug.

She thought about her hot-headed daughter. Michelle's determination had helped her achieve in many pursuits, while her quick tongue had set her up for clashes along the way. But she was as quick to retreat as she was to sally, so rarely stayed out of favor with anybody for long. Elizabeth guessed she could handle Stanley all right.

She moved on to the tomatoes. They were wilted, and the cherry ones were only the size of small grapes. They were thirsty water hogs and she would have to find a mulching system for them next time.

"Hello, good day," came a familiar voice through the thread of her thoughts. She swung around to find Josef standing behind her with a fresh water supply in a bucket.

"Hello, good evening," she replied as she looked at her watch.

"I know," he said with a smile. "I had a good week. I work every day at construction."

"That's great Josef, I'm glad. There's not much to do here today anyway," she continued. She noticed his limp. "What happened you?"

Un bloc m'a frappé. "A block hit me."

"Let's have a look," she said guiding him to a patio chair.

He carefully and painfully took off his sneaker. His toe was red and swollen. A dark, congealed mass of blues and purples lay beneath the raised toenail. His foot was covered in the gray dust of the building site

Je pense que nous avons besoin d'un docteur, "I think we need a doctor," she said.

"Non! Pas un docteur." She looked at him. "Pas un docteur," he repeated lightly. "It's okay."

"It's not okay," she insisted. "But let me wash and bandage it." She went into the house and returned with a bowl of lukewarm soapy water and a clean towel. She washed the toe carefully, using cotton wool to gently debride some of the congealed blood from around the nail bed. He held his toes apart as she wrapped a clean piece of gauze around the wound, finishing with some tape.

"I guess you'll live," she said. "But no more work or walking on it for the rest of the weekend."

"Thank you, thank you, that is much better," he admitted.

"Why did you walk all the way up here?" she asked.

"I no walk." He pointed to the bicycle.

"Oh, very impressive."

He laughed. *Je suis un homme de ma parole,* "I am a man of my word," he continued. *Vous m'attendez. Ainsi je viens.* "You were waiting for me. So I came."

"Yes, you are a man of your word, Josef, and I was expecting you. Come in and have some coffee." They went inside and Elizabeth put on the coffee. Then she handed Josef an application form. "I picked it up from immigration last week. It's a work permit application. We'll fill it out for you to work here and see if we have any luck. It will take some time. You'll need a medical and I'm not sure if they will accept an application from me as your boss."

Josef seemed unconcerned. He looked up and pointed heaven ward. "I will pray."

"And I will pray," she smiled. "How are Marie and Gustaf?"

Bien. Mais la mere est infirme. "Good, but the mother is ill. I visit them tomorrow," he added.

"I thought perhaps you were living with them."

"No, I live close by."

"Is it okay where you live, Josef?"

"No, it's not okay," he said shaking his head and pursing his lips into a wrinkled frown. *Mais à quoi bon se tourmenter,* "But what's the point in tormenting oneself," he added with a laugh.

They finished their coffee in silence. It was a friendly silence, one that required no effort. After a while Josef said, "I go home now."

"One minute." Elizabeth went into her bedroom and returned with a pair of tubular socks and some more gauze. "Wash it every day, *chaque jour.* The socks will protect it."

"Merci! Bonsoir."

"Bonsoir."

~~~

Michelle was in the kitchen, doing the dishes that had stayed heaped in the sink all afternoon. There were ants crawling over the plates, scurrying from her dispassionate flushing of them down the sink. A line of them filed all the way from the sink up the wall, disappearing behind the clock.

Elizabeth came into the kitchen and started to wipe down

the counters with a light bleach. "The only way to keep these ants at bay is to keep the counters scrupulously clean at all times," she said.

"Sorry I didn't get to this sooner, Mom, but I really needed a sleep. I was out of line at lunchtime today. I apologize."

"Yes, well, I was probably being a bit over-protective. But then, that is my job," Elizabeth said with a smile.

"I meant my remark about Josef, that was really out of line. Do you still miss Dad?" she asked.

Elizabeth picked up a tea towel and started to dry the dishes. "That's like asking me, if my right arm was cut off, would I stop missing it after a while," she began. "When your dad died, I mentally couldn't accept it. I would wake up expecting him to be beside me, or I'd answer the phone convinced he would be on the other end. A numbness came over me when I started to realize that he was gone. And for a while I felt nothing."

Michelle rested her hands in the soapy water, and focused her complete attention on her mother. Elizabeth continued.
"Then I started to dream about him. He would come to me in my sleep and we'd be together. I'd have a range of emotions that would stay with me for a time after I woke up. The feelings are staying with me longer and longer. Not all of them are pleasant ones. But they're feelings and I am starting to come alive again." She paused. "But, I will never stop missing him."

"What do you miss the most?"

"This may sound weird to you, Michelle, but I miss the intellectual companionship the most. Someone to share my innermost thoughts with. Someone I know is on the same wavelength. I get so frustrated here at times, and no one seems to think the same way as I do about things. What do you miss the most?" she asked.

"I miss doing fun things with him. But most of all I miss him being part of my life, being there to congratulate me when I do well, and there to pick up the pieces when I bomb out. Like, I wonder what he would think of Stanley. Or any other guy I might hook up with. I rate them all against him, so you don't need to worry about me, Mom. None of them have measured up so far. But I can have fun checking them out, right!"

"Right." Elizabeth gave her daughter a warm hug.

"So the question right now is, will I go all out and wear the dress tonight? Nah," she said with a shake of her head. "Maybe a compromise, dress pants and a blouse." And she headed off to get ready.

~ ~ ~

The nightclub was packed with young people, most of whom knew Stanley. They danced in groups, flirted, and indulged in a bantering dialogue that Michelle could barely understand. There had been some overtures in the car after the dance, but it was packed with friends, all needing a ride home.

Time was not on Stanley's side. Michelle was leaving early next morning. When his taxi duties were completed, it was time to bring her home. They kissed goodbye. It was sweet. But no hearts were broken.

CHAPTER 9

The extension was starting to take shape. The first-floor walls were completed, and the carpenters were busy building the floor for the second story. All internal weight-bearing walls were in place, and the masons were now working on the secondary partitions.

Josef was pleased with the job. It had sustained him for three months now. He had been able to send money back to his mother, buy a bed, and even put some money aside. His toe had long since healed, but Jacques was still his inseparable helpmate and, in turn, Josef was teaching him his trade. But it irked him that he had no work permit. He needed a sponsor, someone who could offer him a job for which no local was qualified or available. He knew after three months that he was needed and rightly should qualify for one. He decided he would approach Robinson at the end of the week.

Lennox was churlish, but had a grudging respect for his workers, and life on the building site had settled into a tolerable routine. Robinson's visits were the main source of angst. He would take delight in finding petty reasons for docking pay, especially amongst the illegals. Because most of the workers had no watches, many of them turned up very early for work, lest they be a few minutes late and incur the wrath of Robinson. But he didn't want anybody on the site except during work hours. When he happened onto the site early himself and there were workers there, he would accuse them of coming early to look for things to steal. The dull expression on the faces of the accused would veil their inner indignation and anger. But to Robinson, this was further evidence for his conviction that the men were a worthless lot he wished he didn't have to deal with.

Four men were in a huddle at lunch break.

Mwen pa vle ou li, "I can't stand him," remarked Claude who had been docked pay that morning for being fifteen minutes late.

Li pran mwen pou yon vie bagay, "He treats me like dirt," choked Jacques, who was always a target for Robinson's displeasure.

Mezanmi nou paka fè anyin anko, kité sa sou kont Bon Dye, "Friends, there is nothing we can do. Leave him to God," advised Josef.

Ke li ale satan! "Let him go to the devil!" Pierre spat in disgust.

They distributed their food, eating in silence now as they each considered how they might mete out justice to Robinson.

Josef could see that his companions were discouraged, and he started to sing a tune that he knew they could not resist. Before long they took the bait. Jacques grabbed two empty paint tins, turned them upside down, and started to tap out a beat with a chisel in one hand and a hammer in the other. The other three flung their arms around each other swaying to the beat and singing at the tops of their voices.

"Look at that! Happy with the simple life," commented a tourist to his companion as they passed by on their rented scooters.

~~~

The men labored hard under an unrelenting blue sky. Water carried cold to the site in the morning was unpalatably tepid by mid-afternoon. The raised structure provided some shade during the morning and late afternoon, but from two to three, the sun poured over the men, pounding them into a joyless silence. T-shirts were damp and clinging; uncovered skin glistened, etched with beaded threads of sweat and grime. By four, the first shadows were cast from the west wall, and by four thirty, with any luck a cooling breeze would slip in through the door and window openings. The tempo and mood would turn up a subtle notch – a snatch of a conversation, a half-whistled tune, and before long revived banter and thoughts of home and a pay check.

Josef put down his float as soon as he saw Robinson's truck wheel in. He wanted to catch him before he started to hand out the payroll. "What do you want?" Robinson asked suspiciously as Josef approached.

"Mr. Robinson, I work here three months, do good work.

You help me get one work permit, please."

"Have you not seen the notices at the Department of Immigration? No more work permits for laboring jobs." He made an X with his arms and swung them wide to bring the point home.

"Mr. Robinson, no Islander here for job, so why no work permit for me?" Josef continued.

Robinson started to bristle. "I don't have time for this shit now, I've got men here waiting for their pay. I'll talk to you next week," he said and brushed his way past Josef.

Josef took his place in the line and Robinson avoided eye contact with him as he handed him his wages. Later, when Josef counted it, there was an amount equal to what the permit holders usually received. This meant a fifty-dollar bonus.

As the men were leaving the work site, Robinson could be seen in deep and heated discussion with Lennox. Josef had an uneasy feeling in his stomach.

~~~

Josef would love to have bought something special with the bonus: a new shirt, perhaps some new shoes. He decided to hold back and put it aside for now. He would splurge on some candies for Marie and Gustaf, though, when he visited them on Sunday.

He stopped at Stan's Corner Store to buy a newspaper. When he was finished in the garden, Elizabeth would help him read it.

~~~

"Hel-lo," he said tunefully as he parked his bike against the wall.

Elizabeth had been lying out on a sun-chair reading a book in the shade. She looked at her watch and jumped out of the chair. She always felt guilty if he caught her resting, knowing that he had already worked a full day before coming up to her. But she had lost track of time and was definitely caught napping.

He handed her the newspaper with a smile. "You read and I work. Then you help me read."

He knew where everything was and had already planned what he was going to do for the next two hours. The grass had grown long around the bushes and needed trimming. The flower patch on the east side needed weeding. And there was, of course, the leaves, always the leaves; fallen from the orange cordia, they needed to be swept up and put in the compost.

Elizabeth opened the newspaper and scanned the pages for headlines that might be of interest. *Piped City Water Promised* read one, referring to a project to supply one of the communities on Flamingo Island. *Tourism: The Lifeblood of the Islands* read another, which suggested severe and swift justice for anyone found guilty of committing a crime against a tourist. *Police Department to Receive More Funding to Fight Crime*, the main targets being drugs and the flow of illegal immigrants.

The crime section included briefs on cocaine, burglary, incest and *More Illegal Haitians*. A forty-foot sloop carrying sixty-three men and women had been intercepted by the marine police and handed over to the immigration authorities.

Elizabeth brooded over what Josef's fate was likely to be. Still no work permit after more than eight months on the island, despite his present long spell of sustained work. The application she had submitted had been put on a waiting list. She had talked with Mrs. Clark about it, who had suggested that he would have a better chance if a native Islander applied for the permit on his behalf. She had promised to let her know if she knew of anyone who could help. She herself had already signed for the Haitian woman who cleaned for her.

Elizabeth scanned the paper for items of interest to share with Josef. Her attention was drawn to a feature on young Islanders, who would be attending an international modeling and talent convention. Perhaps this would be a good starting point, and pictures always helped. He hardly needed to be reminded that the authorities were beefing up their resources to detect and eject him.

She watched him as he raked the leaves, bending and gathering them into a bag, all the while singing softly. She wondered what thoughts his mind held. The maze of language and syntax still sharply divided their worlds. She, who loved to speak her mind, was forced into a barren silence on so many topics.

She got up and went to the kitchen, wondering what she would give him to eat when he was finished. She had taken to giving Josef a meal each Saturday. She wasn't very hungry herself, having attended a farewell luncheon earlier in the day for one of the expats. She was still smarting over an altercation she'd had with Veronica on "the mating habits" of Haitians, and the lengths they would go to get residency status on the islands.

The tirade had echoed a sermon she had heard from one of the local pastors, who cautioned island women not to sell their birthright to foreigners by marrying them. He was referring to "bought" marriages, which were contracted solely to gain resident status for one party and monetary gain for the other. Elizabeth had given the pastor the benefit of the doubt, allowing that any marriage contracted under such conditions was contrary to the laws of God. But she had still felt uneasy as the crowd warmed up to the intensely nationalistic sermon. She had keenly felt her own presence to be somewhat of an intrusion.

Veronica's comments, however, had just hit her as vulgar and ignorant. Elizabeth had waded in on the attack, citing her experience with the Haitian children at school and their close family ties. Grace had cautioned her with a raised eyebrow, and helped steer the conversation into calmer seas. Elizabeth had pulled her horns in, cross with herself for being unable to handle the subject with more adeptness, and also because she had run the risk of marring the festivities. The company very quickly fell into light banter and stories telling of the departing friend's exploits. Nobody seemed to bear any grudges, least of all Veronica, who was the original Annie Oakley, shoot-from-the-lip sort of person.

Grace, who had given her a lift home afterwards, had been conciliatory. "Veronica doesn't think things through before she speaks," she had offered. "She doesn't question the status quo like you do, Elizabeth. But she has a good heart and would be the first in line with provisions if someone's house burnt down."

"I know. It's just that so many of these people live in a twilight zone, their existence barely recognized except as a commodity. It truly makes me heartsick."

"You're right," Grace said, and she warmly squeezed Elizabeth's hand.

The fridge was a sorry sight, half-open bags of carrots, strewn cross-angles to each other. Unnamed plastic containers hid behind juice and milk cartons, and a bowl of cooked Basmati rice took center stage. She cautiously opened the plastic containers, hoping for an easy meal to compliment the rice. One container held last week's salad and the other some tinned pears. The pears were serviceable, but the salad had to go. She took it to the compost, as Josef was turning it.

"Not much to eat in this house tonight, I'm afraid," she said.

He looked at the sky across the east side of the ridge to the sea. "You like fish?"

"Yes."

"I go catch some fish. You come with me. I teach you."

"Okay, let's go," she said happily.

He went to put away the tools and to wash up. She went to put on an old pair of shorts and a T-shirt.

"We have no fishing line or hooks," she said.

"You see," he said with a smile.

"You will see," she corrected him.

"You will see," he repeated.

When they reached the shoreline, he walked north towards an exposed reef. Soon they reached a deep, low cave, gouged out of the limestone cliff that shouldered the eastern coastline. The evening breeze freshened as the sky darkened against a sinking sun. The two figures were silhouetted into a common dusky outline.

Josef disappeared into the cave on his hands and knees, and came out with a reel of fishing line, some lead weights, and two hooks.

They made their way onto the reef. "Careful," Josef cautioned, pointing at a slippery rock. He found a pool with some mollusks in it, and baited both hooks. He swung one of the lines high and wide over the edge of the reef, then handed her the line. "Slowly pull in," he instructed. He then prepared a line for himself and swung it out in a low extended arch, farther out and to the left of hers.

Elizabeth pulled slowly and felt a tug, but it was the lifeless tug of resistant coral. "I'm stuck," she moaned.

"Un moment, I got one!" he said excitedly as he flipped a small grunt onto the rock. He caught it by the tail and smacked its head against the rock, then removed the hook from its senseless body. He looked at her with an expansive beam.

"Okay, show me," he laughed, and she handed him her line. He moved around the reef, changing the angle of the line, giving little tugs to check the resistance as he changed positions. Finally, the line came free and he pulled it in with the hook still intact.

He rebaited both lines, cast them, and gave her one. Before long he had landed another grunt, this time a good-sized one. Elizabeth pulled in an empty line twice and attempted two wild casts, both of which landed about five feet off the reef.

She was just about to start complaining when she felt two tugs that squirmed with life. "I've got one!" she yelled and started pulling it in. He leaned over and placed a hand on the line to assist her. With a quick flip, he landed the angry fish. Its body was bloated and puffed out in a menacing and desperate survival maneuver.

"It's a puffer fish," she wailed. "We can't eat that!"

Josef doubled up in hysterics at her predicament. Meanwhile the fish bounced about the reef, dislodging the hook during its wild gyrations. Josef gently kicked it back over the ledge, whereupon it disappeared to regain its composure.

"I give up," Elizabeth said, laughing and shaking her head.

"No, no I will help you," he insisted. He stopped laughing, but she could see in his eyes he was still very much amused. He rebaited her line and cast it out far. He started to pull it in, indicating the speed and tension she needed and then handed her the line. She continued as instructed, and just as it passed over a coral head she got a bite. It was a strong tug and the gut dug into her skin as it passed over her forefinger. He grabbed the line ahead of her grasp to relieve the tension and helped her in landing it. A foot-long goatfish. The catch of the day!

"Now, we can eat," he said with satisfaction. He dispatched the goatfish with a quick thump across the rock, then strung the three fish together and slung them over his shoulder. They started to make their way back up the ridge in silence.

After a while, Elizabeth put her hand on Josef's shoulder to stop him. "Thank you, Josef," she said. "Thank you for teaching me how to fish."

"You are welcome, Elizabeth," he replied, using her name for the first time.

They continued up the ridge, and he began to sing. He's happy, she thought, he always sings when he's happy.

~~~

Josef cleaned the fish, while Elizabeth prepared a stir-fry to go with the rice.

She opened the cupboard door and beckoned him to have a look at the herbs and spices. "What shall we use on the fish?"

He looked them over, trying to puzzle out what they were, and she got the dictionary to assist. Finally, after much deliberation he opted for paprika, basil, parsley, salt, and pepper. She mixed the herbs with some flour and coated the fish, which he had prepared. She pan-fried them in butter and served them with the rice and vegetables.

"When did you last eat?" she asked, looking at her watch, which now said eight thirty. *"Midi,"* he replied, but didn't elaborate.

She said grace and they started to eat. The fish was extremely tasty, and they congratulated each other on the successful expedition.

After supper, she gave him the paper, and pointed to the models as he read the caption that went with it.

"Which one is most beautiful?" she asked.

He seemed reluctant to choose, but after a while he picked the one dressed in an elegant evening gown, as opposed to the two modeling beach wear.

"I wonder why you are not married, Josef?" she asked.

"Marriage is for men with money," he answered matter-of-factly. But she sensed a bitter tinge to the comment. "When I have money, then I marry."

They looked through more captions, but it was getting late and he was very tired. She lent him her dictionary so that he could continue reading the paper during the week, and watched as he pedaled off into the darkness.

CHAPTER 10

The water in the shallows was tepid as the summer sun continued to raise the temperature on the shelf. Elizabeth swam out about two hundred yards into the cooler, deeper water. Her goggles were leaking, and she had to stop and tread water a number of times to make the necessary adjustments. After much fiddling about, they were finally working well.

As she put her face back into the water, she saw four feet of sleek, menacing silver-gray cross her path about ten feet in front of her. It was patrolling its territory, powerful and assured in its own medium. The barracuda gave her a cold stare as it passed. Then it made a U-turn and quickly came back to check out the intrusion.

Elizabeth was startled, but reassured herself that barracudas were territorial and curious, but rarely aggressive towards swimmers. She turned on her back and started to swim towards shore, propelling herself with strong flipper kicks and deep back-strokes. After about a hundred yards she stopped for a break, sure that she had swum out of the barracuda's territory. She treaded water for about ten seconds, then put her face back in the water to continue her snorkel.

It was coming straight towards her with fixed and staring eyes, mouth slightly open displaying razor sharp teeth. Unnerved, she frantically resumed her swim towards shore, now losing all sense of rhythm. She thrashed her way through the water, spitting the snorkel from her lips. Gulping down desperate draughts of air, she battled her way to the shallows. Finally, she flopped onto the beach, tears of relief mingling with her sea-wet hair and face.

After a while she sat up, and the tears of relief turned to tears of isolation and loneliness as she contemplated her life on the island.

Nine months building shaky bridges to one community, losing her foothold in another, belonging to neither. She was out of her medium. She no longer knew what her medium was. Maybe Grace was right, maybe she needed a breather.

She stood up, put her shorts and T-shirt on, and started to walk aimlessly along the beach. It was deserted. Sunday was a day of worship, and many of the congregations met in the afternoon to avoid the intense heat of the day. Elizabeth had gone to a number of different services, but had no regular church. There was an old Anglican church that was rarely used since the new one had been built, and she sometimes visited it for quiet contemplation. Sally, in the meantime, sent her a steady stream of e-mails, quietly reassuring her and encouraging her to trust the intuition of her soul.

The sand was warm and comforting. She dug her feet in deep, massaging her soles against the gritty coral surface. The afternoon breeze delivered a cooling lick, which would intermittently sweep over her face in a soothing balm.

As she turned rounded the point, she saw a man walking towards her with two children at his side. It was Josef, with Marie and Gustaf. They were returning from church; all three were walking barefoot, their shoes in their hands. What a handsome picture, Elizabeth thought as she looked at them from afar. First at Gustaf, with a clean short-sleeved shirt and brown cotton pants, and then Marie, with a colorful print dress trimmed with pink frills, her hair braided and tied with six pink bows. And finally Josef, dressed in a clean shirt and tie and pressed pants.

"My goodness, don't you all look handsome!" she said, as they approached. They greeted her with appreciative smiles. On their way home from church, they had come down to the beach to take the shortcut home. "How is your mother?" she asked the children.

"She sick, Mrs. Bourke," Gustaf replied.

Elizabeth looked at Josef for confirmation. "Come visit her," he suggested.

She turned and joined them. She was going to have to retrace her steps to get to her bicycle in any case. When they got to the turn-off for their house, Josef suggested that the children go ahead. He would walk with Mrs. Bourke to get her bicycle.

"And where exactly do you live, Josef?" she asked.

"C'est un secret," he said conspiratorially. "Perhaps one day I will show you."

She laughed and left it at that.

"Claire is dying," he said quietly.

Elizabeth picked up her bicycle and they headed back towards the shanties.

~~~

The door was open, and Josef indicated for Elizabeth to go ahead. She hesitated at the step and then went in. There was a narrow wooden cot in the corner, raised about twelve inches off the ground. There were boxes packed neatly with clothes, and two bedrolls in the far corner. On the wall hung the dress Claire had worn to the Christmas concert.

Claire was lying awkwardly on the cot, propped up with an old sofa cushion. She was covered with a faded and patched sheet. Her breath came in wheezes, yet she managed a smile of recognition for Elizabeth. The smell of urine and bile pervaded the air. A bucket at the end of the bed contained the sum of Claire's daily bodily functions. Gustaf took it outside to empty it in the latrine.

"She should be in hospital, Josef," Elizabeth said.

"She has no money. She worry for her children," Josef responded. "The nurse come to see her."

"Josef, ask her if she would like to come and stay with me for a while, with the children."

Josef looked at Elizabeth's ashen face. "Are you sure?" he asked.

"Ask her."

When he did, Claire quietly nodded her assent.

"Pack your things, Gustaf and Marie. I will be back at six to pick you up. Will you be here to help?" she asked Josef.

"I will be here," he replied.

~ ~ ~

"Are you sure you know what you're doing?" Grace asked. "This may be more than you can handle."

"No, I'm not sure," Elizabeth confessed. "But we'll manage. I can't leave her and the children in that situation. I just can't. I've called the hospital and they've agreed to send a nurse to check on her every second day."

"And I can pop in while you're at school," Grace offered.

"The hospital said she won't live for more than a week or two. I'm bringing her home to die in comfort, and to be there for the children."

"What happened to the old aunt?"

"Aunt Jessie moved to one of the other islands two months ago to find work. All the neighbors except Josef are keeping their distance."

~~~

When Elizabeth and Grace reached the shanty, the children were both sitting on a box of clothes outside the door. Their mother was sitting on the doorstep, and Josef was standing beside her. They were all washed and ready to go.

Elizabeth smiled at Claire. She bent down on one side of her and wrapped an arm around her. Josef wrapped his arm around her other side, and clasped Elizabeth's arm as they very slowly walked her to the car. Meanwhile, Grace had packed the children's belongings into the trunk, and had seated Gustaf in the front seat and Marie in the back. Elizabeth slid in beside Marie, and Claire collapsed in beside her.

"I will follow on my bicycle," Josef said.

As they drove away from the shanty, Elizabeth saw Claire looking at her home for the last time: the shambles of leaning shacks and corrugated fencing, the fishnet hammock swinging aimlessly under the orange cordia trees, and the wooden bench tilting forward on shaky legs. One large, silent tear slowly rolled down her cheek. Elizabeth took her hand and caressed it as they quietly made their way up Ridge Road.

Marie and Gustaf were first out of the car, eyes wide with anticipation. They studied the white picket fence and the neat white house with its green corrugated roof. They looked at Elizabeth, waiting for instructions.

"Tell your mom we will wait for Josef before taking her out of the car. You stay with her, Marie, and Gustaf can help me bring in the boxes."

Grace opened the trunk. She took out a cooler and gave it

to Elizabeth. "Supper," she said. "I didn't think you would have time to cook."

Elizabeth gave her a powerful hug.

"Oh, don't be such a mush, Elizabeth, it's only chili and corn bread."

"You're a good friend, Grace."

"And you're a very courageous one."

Elizabeth led Gustaf into the spare bedroom. There were two made-up single beds in it. "We'll put you and Marie in here," she said. "And your maman will stay in my bedroom, where I can keep an eye on her."

"Josef is here," Grace hollered from the kitchen.

Elizabeth went out to meet him, and they carefully assisted Claire inside.

"In my room," said Elizabeth, nodding toward the open bedroom door. The double bed had clean sheets on it and four pillows. A futon mattress was on the floor in one corner and a commode, borrowed from the hospital, was at one side of the bed. They placed Claire on the bed. She rolled with pleasure into the comfort of a deep, well-sprung mattress, her emaciated body appreciating the cushioning it provided.

"You rest awhile, Claire, and later on we will bring you some supper." Josef translated into Creole.

Mèsi, she replied. *Mwen pa mange. Ban mwen yon boison, tanpri.* "I'm not hungry. But I would like a drink, please." She sunk down into the pillows and closed her eyes as they quietly left the room.

The children were climbing on their beds and sorting out their various spaces. Elizabeth showed them which drawers they could use and which ones were full of Michelle's Caribbean gear.

"Two lights, one by each bed. No excuses for not having homework done," she said with a grin.

They went into the kitchen, to find Grace organizing things and putting the chili in the oven to reheat. "Supper should be ready in twenty minutes. I've got to go," she said.

After supper, Elizabeth asked Josef to help her write out a list of phrases in Creole, which she and Grace could use to communicate with Claire. Phrases related to eating, sleeping, comfort, toileting. Then she gave Josef a copy of *The Healing Prayer* in French and asked him to translate it into Creole.

"What do you think?" she asked. "Would Claire like this?"

C'est une priere trés efficace, trés forte, "It's a very effective, strong prayer," he said, and nodded his head.

CHAPTER 11

Her breathing was shallow and it bubbled out through waterlogged lungs. Every moan was amplified, echoing in Elizabeth's sensitized ear. God! When will it end? Elizabeth thought, as she recalled the past two weeks. The first week had been grueling physically – washing, cleaning and assisting Claire, on top of a normal school day, as well as caring for the children. But it had been well worth the effort, as Elizabeth witnessed a cloud of fear and anxiety lift from both the children and Claire. Free from the grind of daily survival, the children had been able to spend worry-free time with their mother. They showed off their schoolwork and sang her favorite songs. Grace had come each day to sit with Claire for an hour or two and to bring her lunch, though Claire ate very little.

But the nights had been long. Claire's every breath was drawn in with uncertainty, and every breath exhaled slowly released her of her life of burden. This had brought Elizabeth to the very vortex of the dark tunnel into which Claire proceeded. Memories of her last days with Matt came in waves, purging her of her last vestiges of self-pity, and steeling her against the pounding forces of the human tragedy of which she was now a part. Most nights, she had spent hours attending to Claire when she became distressed, either sitting and holding her hand, or praying quietly with her, each in her own tongue. She started the day at five thirty in the morning by assisting Claire on the commode and giving her a sponge bath. The children would then spend some time with their mother, while Elizabeth prepared breakfast and a lunch to take to school.

By the time Josef arrived on the following Saturday, Elizabeth looked pale and exhausted. He had taken one look at her and pleaded with her to sleep for a few hours in the children's room while he was there to keep an eye on things. She had complied without protest and had fallen into a black hole of sleep that severed all ties with the contingent world.

When she finally awoke, it was in response to a knock on

the bedroom door. "Come in." She sat up and came to a full and refreshed consciousness.

Marie peered expectantly, around the door. "She's awake!" she shouted excitedly. "Come on, Gustaf."

Gustaf appeared carrying a tray of tea and toast, and an orange.

"Wow!" Elizabeth exclaimed. "Have I slept that long? Is it Sunday?"

"Yes, it's Sunday," they laughed.

"Your mother, how is your mother?" she asked, alarmed.

"She's fine," came a male voice from the doorway, and Elizabeth looked up to see Josef standing there with a cup of tea in his hand. "Can I come in?"

"Please," she replied, after a quick body scan had revealed that she was fully clothed.

He sat on the opposite bed and looked at her with soft gentle eyes, revealing part worry, part tenderness, and a hint of amusement.

"What?" she exclaimed, as she read their final quality.

J'étais resté toute la nuit dans votre chambre, "I stayed all night in your bedroom." He hesitated and then added, "Avec Claire."

"And where were the children?" she asked.

"We all slept in your bedroom," Marie interjected. "It's very big."

"It's an invasion!" Elizabeth had exclaimed, and she sipped some tea to give herself time to fully interpret the situation. Veronica would have a field day with this one – if she ever found out. Appearances were all, and yet things were rarely as they appear to be. Finally, she burst out laughing. The children laughed, too, but Josef retained his composure, all the time keeping his attention on Elizabeth.

"Go visit your maman," he suggested, and they both left obediently. "You were asleep."

"You could have woken me up," she said gently.

"No, I not wake you," he said shaking his head. "I stay tonight," he added.

She looked at him in disbelief.

"Let me help you," he insisted.

"Okay, I surrender," she agreed.

The next morning he had quietly left while Elizabeth was attending to Claire.

~~~

The following week had seen Claire descend, from feeble but mentally alert, to a semi-conscious state and complete physical breakdown. She needed help turning in the bed and could no longer use the commode. The nurse had taken it away and left a bunch of incontinent pads in its place. Not that Claire had much to deposit; she now only took sips of juice or lukewarm milky tea, intermittently throughout the day.

Grace had been a stalwart, coming faithfully each day.

~~~

It was now Friday and Elizabeth felt sure that Claire couldn't hold on much longer. She couldn't understand why she was still struggling – as if every minute, however tortuous, was worth the effort.

Suddenly, Claire opened her eyes in a wild stare, like an underwater swimmer surfacing for air. Slow comprehension of her surroundings, of Elizabeth, seemed to reassure her. But she also seemed to be looking for someone…something. Elizabeth wondered if she should bring the children into the bedroom to be with her. It was nine in the evening. The children had just gone to bed. Then Claire relaxed in response to a gentle hand and arm massage, and slowly sank back down into her murky waters.

Elizabeth continued her vigil, accompanied by the well-worn little brown book that Sally had sent her months ago.

O Son of Man
Thou art My dominion and My dominion perisheth not; wherefore fearest thou thy perishing? Thou art My light and My light shall never be extinguished; why dost thou dread extinction? Thou art my robe and My robe shall never be outworn. Abide then in thy love for Me, that thou mayest find Me in the realm of glory.

At five in the morning Claire awoke with a keen and focused alertness. She spoke slowly but urgently. She wanted to see Josef. Elizabeth nodded and went to wake up the children.

"Where does Josef live?" she asked Gustaf.

"He live in the old house on the beach, down by where you met us." Elizabeth had a vague recollection of an old abandoned beach house, which was at the north end of the beach.

"Stay with your mother, I will be back as soon as I can."

The morning air was fresh and invigorating and she sped down the ridge in double time. It was still dark, but the blackness had a dusky hue that promised to dissipate with the advancing sun.

The stillness up on the ridge contrasted with a stirring down in Little Haiti. People were taking advantage of the early morning coolness, to wash and prepare for the day. They watched silently as Elizabeth made her way through the clutter of sheds and shanties. Some raised a hand in greeting, some smiled, others stared in bewilderment. As she approached the lane that led to the beach house, she hesitated momentarily. Then she crossed an invisible boundary and continued her journey with single-minded intent. As she turned the corner, the house suddenly came into view. The dilapidated remnants of somebody's vacation dream home showed very little signs of occupancy. Windows, doors, steps – all were broken and the strewn remains were scattered on the ground. Part of one gable end was missing, revealing an inside room. Elizabeth slowly walked around the outside, looking for signs of life. On the seaward side, she spotted a bicycle hidden in the gutted remains of what would once have been the kitchen. It was Josef's.

She climbed the broken steps and called softly as she knocked on the door. "Josef, are you there? It's Elizabeth."

He opened the door and took her arm, pulling her inside quickly.

"People see you come here?" he asked.

"I don't think so," she replied uneasily.

He smiled and released her. His face was shaved on one side and soaped on the other. He stood in a pair of boxer shorts. *Il y a une grande rumeur qui circule, l'immigration prepare le prison pour les Haitians sans les permits de travail.* "There is a big rumor that immigration is preparing the prison for the Haitians without work permits. We must be very careful," he explained as he quickly put on some pants.

"Claire is asking for you," Elizabeth said as she looked around the room. The inside was transformed. It was freshly painted, and the floor was swept clean. There was a small table and chair in one corner and a bed in another. Two bookshelves displayed a modest collection of books, and a paraffin lamp. On the table was a basin of water propping up a mirror, and some soap and a razor.

"Okay, let me finish and then I come," Josef said. He moved the chair out for her, and she sat and watched him in silence.

"It's not much," he remarked as he patted his face dry and opened the small built-in closet he had repaired. He selected a clean T-shirt and showed it to her for her approval. She smiled and nodded, but her throat convulsed and a large, uninvited tear forced its way over her lower eyelid down her cheek. She wiped it quickly and self-consciously with her thumb.

Josef offered her his hand as she rose from the chair. "Listen, you go and I follow you," he said, still holding her hand. He squeezed it lightly before releasing it. "It will be okay," he assured her. She regained her courage and stepped out into the dawn.

She pedaled hard to quickly put distance between her and his refuge, keenly aware of the danger she had placed him in. She struggled up the ridge, but gave in before the summit and walked the last piece. The dawn chorus was in full swing: birds chirped, roosters crowed, and a donkey brayed a loud sonorous wake-up call in the distance.

She rounded the turn into her yard, dumped the bicycle unceremoniously on the grass, and sprinted towards the house.

Claire was asleep with Marie lying beside her. Gustaf was in his own bed, fast asleep. Five minutes later, Josef turned up and she brought him immediately into the bedroom.

He placed his hand on Claire's brow and called to her. *Leve sè mwen. Mwen bezwen pale avek ou. Leve sè mwen* "Wake up, sister. I need to talk with you. Wake up, sister."

Claire was drawn to consciousness as if by a magnet. She slowly opened her eyes. *Mwen malade. Mwen fatigue. Mwen pral mouri.* "I am sick. I am tired. I am dying." She rested, then pursed and rolled her lips, to distribute the scant supply of saliva. Elizabeth brought her some water to sip. She refused it. *Mwen pral kite timoun yo nan min ou wap veye yo.* "I leave my children in your care."

Josef translated for Elizabeth, who nodded her ascent.

Pa okipe-ou. Nou va pran swen yo. "Don't worry. We will take care of them." She offered a weak smile. *Sè mwen an rete Milot. Li rele Françoise Louima.* "My sister lives in Milot. Her name is Françoise Louima." *Bondye va beni ou.* "May God bless you." She sunk back into a listless state.

"I must go," Josef said. "I am late for work." He left without further comment.

CHAPTER 12

Josef arrived at the site just in time to see Robinson disappear in a cloud of dust. The rest of the men were gathered in a low murmuring huddle.

"Sak pase?" he inquired, as he rested his bicycle against the tool shed.

Lennox approached him with an anxious scowl. "Immigration went to de far site yesterday. Dey catch four Haitians without permits. Mr. Robinson expect dem here Monday. Everybody to work all day Saturday and Sunday. Next week Haitians without work permit stay off de site."

"Maybe, we go home now," Josef suggested.

"Not if you want de week's pay," Lennox replied, raising the briefcase Robinson had left. "What are you all staring at? Get to work!" he challenged the huddle of men as he swept past them on his way to the office to secure the payroll. The men slowly dissipated and distributed themselves at their customary positions.

Jacques brought Josef his tools. *Yo te arete kousin mwen yè.* "They arrested a cousin of mine last night," he said as he laid down a palate of freshly mixed mortar beside him. *Fam nan te ale nan yon rage. Li gross.* "His wife has fled to the bush. She's pregnant." Josef nodded his condolences. *Anpil brik, Jacques,* "More bricks, Jacques," he said. Josef sandwiched the bricks between smooth sweeps of red-tinged mortar. The bricks edged the window lintels, echoing faded colonial splendor. *Ki kan timoun nan ap fèt?* "When is the baby due?"

Nan yon mwo. "In one month."

A le pran nivo, Jacques. "Get the level, Jacques."

Jacques sidled towards the tool shed, furtively checking for unusual vehicles or activity. The further he walked from Josef, the more anxious he seemed. He grabbed the level from the shelf and quickly returned to Josef's side.

Si yo vini pa gen koté pou ou kouri. Paske yo kon-nen nou tout deja, Jacques. Moun-n yo pa bezwen nou, yap arete yo, e, yap voye yo nan peyi yo. "If they come, there is no point in running. They know us all, Jacques. When they do not need us, they will arrest us and send us back to our country."

Mwen pa gen kote pou mwen rete, "I have no country," responded Jacques. *Fanmi-y moin reté nan yon chan kan-n Republik St. Domingue*" "My family are all on a sugar plantation in the Dominican Republic."

Kay ou se nan kè ou li ye. Ou gen bon kè. "You carry your home in your heart. You have a good heart."

The sun rose high in the sky and forced its intensity through the solid layer of cement, which marked the flat-roofed second story. Those working on the first floor steadily absorbed the heat until their skins glistened. Brows were mopped with shirt ends or bandanas, and the fear of capture was dulled by the immediacy of staying cool, drinking water, and continuing the day's labor. Lunch break was cut down to a half hour, when shade was more coveted than nourishment and those skilled in the technique of instant cat-napping found thirty minutes of reprieve.

At four in the afternoon, a black Honda Civic with tinted windows drove past the site slowly. Lennox was checking angles and levels. Josef was using his index finger to smooth out a corner he had just mortared. Only the highly sensitized Jacques noticed it out of his peripheral vision, but even he discounted it after an untroubled thirty minutes had elapsed.

Cooling breezes swept into the site at five, elevating the mood as time moved inexorably towards shut down and a pay check at six. The Honda Civic lurked out of sight on a knoll overlooking the site. As the men lined up in an expectant group outside the office, a signal was given. Two white vans displaying immigration decals quickly appeared, followed immediately by two police cars that blocked off the exit routes. A loud voice from the loudspeaker of one of the police cars advised the men to identify themselves and produce their work permits. The swoop was quick and efficient: six illegals were picked up and bundled into the waiting vans. Lennox was issued with an order to appear before the courts for hiring people without work permits. The rest of the workforce stood in numbed silence as they watched their compatriots being driven away. A silent and ashen Lennox paid the remaining men, closed up the office, and headed off in the direction of

Robinson's house.

Thirty minutes after the site had been cleared, a terrified Jacques emerged from the outhouse. His nervous bowels had sent him packing in that direction, minutes before the swoop had occurred. He took the bicycle he now shared with Josef and started to cycle away from town and up towards the ridge. He would spend the next several nights in the bush.

~ ~ ~

Elizabeth was in automatic mode. She had been here before and she knew how attention to detail could keep a sea of emotion at bay, as miraculously as the little Dutch boy's finger in the dike pushed back the North Sea. She called the hospital and the morgue, and sent word to Aunt Jessie in West Island. She would have to transport the body herself. Grace's jeep was too small, so she called Charlie, her affable, but rarely seen, house agent. He appeared two hours and five beers later with a piece of carpet lining the back of his truck. Between them they hoisted the shrouded corpse of Claire into the back of the truck. The children, who were with Grace, were spared this spectacle.

The mortician, an underpaid hospital orderly, received the remains without ceremony and asked Elizabeth to sign the papers saying that the next-of-kin would not be claiming the body. This relegated Claire to a pauper's burial, which would be paid for by the state. Elizabeth went to speak to the pastor of the church that the children had attended with Josef. They agreed on a quiet service on Monday morning, and he would announce it at church on Sunday. She then phoned Mrs. Clark to explain to her that neither she nor the children would be at school on Monday.

The frenzy of activity kept her from registering Josef's absence – until Sunday morning when the children wondered if he would be coming to take them to church. She quietly dressed the children and walked with them down the ridge, fully expecting to see Josef when she got to the church. She noticed his green bicycle propped in the bicycle rack as she entered the church, the cocooned retreat of the Haitian exile: a world where dignity and hope were restored for brief interludes, where Creole triumphed over broken, faltering English; a place where faith was replenished and donned like a suit of armor and buffed to a shine by the admonitions and incantations of the earnest preacher.

Elizabeth understood very little of what was going on, and took her cues to sit, stand, and clap from the children. The nest of familiarity for the congregation was a jumbled maze of messages to Elizabeth, which she could only decode in snatches. She understood that what she was experiencing today was the negative of the picture that these people faced every day. Some of the songs had a familiar lilt to them, the ones that Josef habitually hummed or sang while working. She scanned the crowd for him, but the sea of closely shaved black male heads gave few clues.

After the service, a number of tearful women came up to the children and embraced them. Elizabeth stood at the bottom of the steps keeping a close eye on the green bicycle. A young man not much older than eighteen came to claim it.

"Wait!" she cried, making a lunge to intercept him. *Cette bicyclette est à Josef, n'est ce pas?* "This is Josef's bicycle, isn't it?" The young man looked at her, barely fighting back tears.

Il est pris, "He is taken," he blurted out.

The reality of the situation struck her like a thunderbolt, and she stood transfixed to the spot for several minutes while the young man rambled on in incomprehensible Creole. *Où est il maintenant?* "Were is he now?" she finally demanded.

À la prison. Demain on le renvoyera en Haïti. "In prison. Tomorrow they will send him back to Haiti."

~ ~ ~

A large group of people, much larger than Elizabeth had expected, were gathered around the gray-brown rectangular hole. Who were they, she wondered, and where were they when Claire really needed them?

A lot of voices spoke in Creole, but there was a small group, slightly to one side who chattered in English. Mrs. Clark was in that group, and Elizabeth would learn later that a number of Island women whom Claire had done ironing and washing for, accounted for some of the others.

Elizabeth was taken aback at first by the intense outpouring of grief that accompanied the simple burial service. Sonorous wailing, followed by swooning and swaying came in repeated waves, providing palpable energy to the coldest and most lifeless of deeds – the interment of human remains to the belly of the earth. But soon she was carried aloft by the emotional torrent. Spiritually, she drifted to another sphere, while her drained physical persona remained at the graveside, weeping for losses far greater than the one being committed to the earth that day.

Part II

CHAPTER 13

The policeman nodded, and then uttered a low grunt to beckon the next passenger forward with her bags. Some jewelry had been reported stolen, and all the baggage that had been checked on the plane bound for Cap Hatien was now being inspected for it. The soft-spoken, courteous security officer had been replaced by the regular police for the search.

Elizabeth's backpack had been given a cursory inspection and put back on the loading trolley. The bag now on display was being thoroughly plundered. Its contents – underwear, sheets, pillow cases, and toiletries – ballooned out of the unzipped bag like popped corn.

Gustaf and Marie sat frozen to their seats in wide-eyed wonder, as they gulped in the noisy scene of expectant travelers, laden with the small comforts afforded them after months of toil. The travelers were now wrestling with suitcases, bags, and parcels, all precariously overloaded and ill-equipped to weather an intrusive inspection and re-packing. The atmosphere was laced with tension and suspicion.

"Where you get dem bracelets?" the policeman demanded as he uncovered a small box with two gold chain bracelets neatly curled on some cotton wool.

"I bought them. They are gifts for my sisters."

"Where you wo'kin?"

"Club Med."

"How you can afford these on money you make?"

The woman looked him full in the eye, proud and with dignity. "I work hard and spend my money as I choose."

She had been here ten years, long enough to apply for permanent resident status, and was no longer willing to be arbitrarily pigeon-holed into perpetual poverty. As she spoke her eyes softened and her elegant face lit up into a disarming smile.

The officer met her penetrating gaze, and a shadow of embarrassment spread from his eyes through his cheeks to his

ear lobes. "Okay, Ma'am, you done. Next!"
Next in line for inspection were the stuffed boxes of an older man. His hunched shoulders visibly straightened as he listened to his compatriot's courageous stance. The officer audibly sighed as he eyed the tightly packed and taped boxes.
"Toys for my little grandchildren," said the old man as he flashed the officer a hopeful toothless grin."
"Okay, okay. Next." The flicker of a smile momentarily pinched his cheeks as he shook his head in an act of resignation. Those close enough to witness laughed and the atmosphere was gradually drained of its charge and light banter filled the vacuum. Eventually, all the luggage and carry-ons had been checked, and the mélange of bags, sacks, and suitcases, now plastered and buttressed with duct tape, strings, and belts, was hoisted back onto the thirty-four-seat plane.
Elizabeth was ushered up to the coveted front seats by the smiling flight attendant. Unsure of whether the preferential treatment was due to her two small wards or her solitary whiteness, she timidly but graciously accepted. She looked around warily, lest she be met with hurt disapproval, but was greeted with nods and smiles. There was good-humored curiosity about the white woman traveling to Haiti with two small children.
Marie tensed as the engines roared into action, while Gustaf jammed his nose against the window eagerly. Elizabeth took Marie's hand and began to tell her the story of the magical goose that flew across the ocean to rescue a brother and sister from the wicked witch, and bring them home to the land of mountains and streams where bananas and mangos grew in people's yards.
"In preparation for take off, please fasten your seat belts," the flight attendant announced. Elizabeth wondered how many of the passengers could understand the instructions, so clearly formulated in English. Not that any seasoned traveler ever paid any attention to these pre-flight monologues, and a quick glance around the cabin indicated the usual disinterest among this batch of travelers. Still, she wondered how the attendant would cope with a true emergency when almost all of her passengers were fluent only in Creole.

"...And the goose had a saddle made of golden braid, with horns of ivory, studded with emeralds. The goose told the boy and his little sister to hang onto the horns. They grasped the horns tightly as the great white bird launched herself into the clear blue sky and winged her flight to the South. The little girl opened her eyes and looked down over the deep blue ocean...."

"Look, Marie, a ship, I see a ship!" Gustaf cried.

Marie slowly released her grip on Elizabeth and shifted forward to see what her brother had spotted. He broke into Creole and launched into his own fairytale of what the ship was carrying and where it was bound.

Elizabeth closed her eyes, savoring the brief respite. Her thoughts drifted to Josef and the message he had sent to her the night before he was due to be deported. She had then phoned up Stanley Robinson's father, who was a government minister, pointing out that there was an application submitted for Josef's work permit and recounting his virtues and talents. The minister was polite, but had made no promises other than that he would look into it. Later that night she had received a call from an immigration officer who had agreed that if Josef's flight was paid for, he could leave the country without a formal deportation stamp on his passport. This meant that he could apply for re-admittance if he got a work permit some time in the future. In the meantime, she could visit him at the police station if she wished. It had been ten in the evening by the time she was able to free herself of funeral arrangements and have Grace come to stay with the children.

The holding cell was a small, foul-smelling, unlit building, separated from the main complex by a narrow alleyway. Its only means of lighting was the open barred door, which faced the sidewall of the police station across the alley. The cell had two cots and four prisoners, three of them Haitians awaiting deportation. The fourth occupant was a well-known Islander whose mental swings were notorious. He was a regular overnighter whenever his exploits got out of hand. When he arrived he made loud protestations of hunger and general discomfort, and was quick to ask Elizabeth to please get some soda and cigarettes for him.

Josef had appeared out of the dark recesses of the cell and

held the bars of the door as Elizabeth came closer. She could see two other men behind him in the darkness, one lying on the bare concrete floor, the other barely visible except for the whites of his eyes in the far corner. The loquacious nut was reclining on the cot, holding forth like a Roman patrician. He was the son of so-and-so and the nephew of some other high-ranking official.

"You go by my daddy house, Miss," he said to Elizabeth. "You see where he live. I ain't go to stay in this piss hol'. No, Sir!"

Josef raised an eyebrow in his direction and cracked a wry smile at Elizabeth. But she could see the pain in his eyes. She curved her hands over his in a comforting embrace, as she recounted the leeway he was being afforded. He nodded his resignation.

They talked for a short time about the children. He would contact the sister in Milot to let her know of Claire's death and that the children would be arriving in a few weeks. He would then head on to Gonaives or Port au Prince to try and find work. He gave Elizabeth the address of a cousin in Gonaives where he could be contacted, but there was no telephone. Elizabeth could feel the stare of the policeman focused on their intertwined fingers like a hot beam, and she slowly slid her hands down.

"You go now," he suggested softly. "I will be okay. I am in God's hands."

That was the last she had seen or heard of him....

"Tante Elizabeth, look, it's Haiti!"

She looked out the window as the plane made a curving sweep to the right, bringing both the seafront and the backdrop of mountains into view at once. A number of wooden sloops could be seen plying through the murky red-brown waters that seeped out from the harbor front and river delta. The advance of brown water was brought to an abrupt halt where it met the deeper blue of the ocean. Two large rust-encrusted cargo vessels were in port.

Elizabeth's eye was diverted to the panoramic view of mountains, which came looming into the foreground as the plane started its descent to Cap Hatien. Houses were perched precariously in clusters on the steep slopes. They appeared to be made out of plain concrete blocks, and were stark and gray. Immediately below, the wide, flat flood plain was dotted with more houses, squatting on the mud, unaware of their tenuous grasp on terra firma.

The plane banked and straightened up for its final approach. Green, fertile fields with a variety of animals and an assortment of wooden and wattle dwellings marked the approach. The open runway came into view. Its broad grassy borders were littered with washing, spread out to dry by the many people who were freely walking, talking, and carrying on their business, within feet of the concrete runway. A cluster of sheds marked the airport terminal.

The plane came to a stop, and an eager group of baggage handlers quickly made their way out on the runway. Elizabeth fell in line with the crowd pressing its way towards the immigration desk. She fished in her bag for the envelope containing Claire's death certificate, the children's Haitian birth certificates, and a letter from Aunt Jessie giving custody of the children to Elizabeth for the duration of the trip. The immigration officer was unimpressed with her documentation, and started to barrage her with questions about the children's health, their HIV status, the father's whereabouts.

Elizabeth's French faltered during the explanation of Aunt Jessie's connection to the family and her authority to leave the children in Elizabeth's care.

"Excuse me, can I help?" came a quiet, assured voice over her shoulder.

It was the woman who had the bracelets at the airport. Elizabeth gave her a quick synopsis of the circumstances leading up to her trip to Haiti. The woman started to litigate on her behalf, and before long, the officer stamped Elizabeth's passport and ushered them through.

"Welcome to Haiti," the woman said. "Where are you staying?"

Elizabeth told her that she had booked into Le Roi Christophe for that night, but planned on heading to Milot the following day.

"We can share a taxi, if you like."

"Yes, please," Elizabeth replied gratefully.

They picked up their bags from customs, and as they left the compound Elizabeth was immediately swarmed by money changers offering the best rates for her U.S. dollars, along with children who were also looking for dollars. "Miss, give me one dollar," came a chorus of voices, as they pressed their ragged little bodies and eager faces closer to her. She had her backpack secured to her back, and Marie and Gustaf were firmly attached to each side carrying their own small suitcases that she had bought them before leaving. Elizabeth hesitated, wondering if she should stop and check in her purse for change, but her newfound friend cautioned her not to stop, to keep walking.

Soon they were all huddled inside a ramshackle old beater that was posing brazenly as a taxi. Had she been on her own, Elizabeth would certainly never have gotten into it. As they made their way through the crowded streets, it weaved through and around obstacles, beeping its horn with monotonous regularity.

The two women introduced themselves. Claudette told Elizabeth that she had formerly been a teacher in Haiti, but had lost hope in the government school system. She had been waitressing on the Islands now for over ten years, and her salary and tips were putting her two younger sisters through private school and hopefully on to university. "U.S. dollars go a long way in Haiti," she added.

When they arrived at the hotel, the driver asked Elizabeth for ten U.S. dollars for her part of the fare. Claudette quickly intervened and beat him down to seven dollars each, including the extra mile to her home.

"Here is my parents' phone number. If you need help, call me."

"Thanks, you've been a great help."

The room had a large double bed against one wall and a single bed against the opposite wall. A recessed window overlooked the narrow street below. The sheets were of pure white cotton with embroidered trim, and the dark wood of the bed echoed back to the colonial splendor of the hotel's past. It had once hosted Napoleon's sister Pauline, during its time as the French Governor's residence.

It was a large, expansive bed and Elizabeth submitted herself to the soft indulgence it offered. Tomorrow was going to be a journey into an uncertain future. She could afford one night in the goose fairy's palace before returning the children to the mountains beyond.

Gustaf stood on the single bed, his elbows stretched out on the ample sill, craning out the open window and drinking in the sights, sounds, and smells of his country. A country of which he knew nothing, save the stored memories and vignettes passed on by his mother.

Marie, fragile and bewildered by her constantly changing circumstances, curled up in the bed beside Elizabeth.

"Okay, ma petite, let's finish our story and then you must go to sleep."

CHAPTER 14

Marie and Gustaf sat eating their breakfast on the open veranda by the lobby, which served as a dining area. Elizabeth was at the front desk trying to figure out the easiest and cheapest way to get to Milot, twenty-five kilometers to the north. She could either take the easy way or the cheap way, but not both. The easy way was an expensive taxi ride; the cheap way was by tap-tap.

As Elizabeth pondered her options, a young man approached her and introduced himself as Bernard. "I am a friend of Claudette's. I would like to be your guide and assist you to find the children's aunt. I can speak English, French, and Creole," he said.

Elizabeth didn't need much convincing. The travel handbook she had consulted had advised using a local guide, especially for traveling off the tourist track. "Come and join us for breakfast and we can talk," she offered.

Over breakfast, Bernard explained that he made his living from guiding people, as well as helping some local companies with translation work. He usually went to the airport every day to check for travelers, but yesterday he'd had some other work to attend to. For the next few days he was free, though, and totally at her disposal. They agreed on a daily rate of thirty U.S. dollars – cheap by Elizabeth's standards, but a windfall for the young man.

Bernard went on to recount his life story to her. His father had died when he was eight and he had joined a crowd of street kids who frequented the airport each day. A white missionary, who had taught him English, French, and survival skills, had taken him in. He was now married and had one child. He, like so many more Elizabeth would meet, was hoping to find a less precarious existence in another country.

"Do you want me to look for a cheap taxi, or do you want to take the tap-tap?" he asked.

"Tap-tap," the children piped up in unison. They had, until now, been silent but attentive throughout the exchange.

"Tap-tap it is," Elizabeth confirmed.

Bernard smiled approvingly. "Haitian way, that's good," he

said diverting his attention to the children and talking to them in Creole.

Elizabeth took the opportunity to check out and pay the bill. "Okay, *allons nous*," she directed, and the little company marched out through the walled courtyard and into the mass of humanity which filled the streets below.

The sidewalk outside the hotel had a thick layer of encrusted and decaying garbage on it. Bernard walked on the street, which was cleaner, and thus avoided weaving around the groups of people who had set up stands on the sidewalks. A shoe shiner looked up at Elizabeth from his street corner. Her leather sandals dashed his hopes of a job that might have tipped handsomely. But he smiled at her anyway and bade her "*Salut.*" Bernard stayed in front, checking out the intersections for traffic before they crossed.

They made their way through narrow, winding streets, gradually leaving the brightly-colored street facades behind. They entered into a quarter of gloomy decay, where paint had peeled and wood had taken on the pall of filth and neglect. As they crossed an old wooden bridge, they moved to another place and time – to a country cut adrift in the Caribbean, suspended in isolation between the resonance of an African heritage and the inescapable dependence on an uncaring Western world.

Elizabeth's senses were assailed from every side. There were smells of wet earth tinged with rotting matter, laced with the more savory scents of stews simmering over charcoal burners. There were the sounds of bartering, of a thousand foot beats, of pigs, and chickens, and of the ever-present press of humanity on every side.

Finally, Bernard stopped beside a row of colorful pickup trucks, slowly being filled with people and produce.

"This one's going to Milot." Bernard pointed to one that was half-full.

They clambered on the back and found space on the simple benches bolted in place around the sides. At first the other passengers made way, providing ample room for the *blanche*, who, it was assumed, needed more space than everyone else. But as space became a premium, her whiteness became incidental. She was soon intertwined amongst the bodies, with one arm around Marie and the other around, but not touching, a neat little man pressed up against her on the other side. They nodded to each other in tacit agreement that their cramped quarters were acceptable. Gustaf was sitting on a pile of rice sacks and crates of soda pop. Bernard had seated himself on the roof of the truck with two other men, their legs drooping in Elizabeth's field of vision. Elizabeth smiled at the woman opposite her. The truck sputtered and then roared into gear, lurching forward to begin its expedition to Milot.

As it rattled through the streets the children loosened up. Marie's grip on Elizabeth became less insistent and Gustaf gazed at each passenger in turn with open curiosity. Any foreign propriety and reserve was soon also shaken from Elizabeth's manner. She found herself drinking in the atmosphere and looking into the eyes of her fellow passengers; they returned her gaze with mutual curiosity and acceptance. She could smell the body odor of the man next to her - not unclean but emitting a musky scent drawn forth from his body core by the heat of the day. His wife pinched closer to him on the other side, and performed little grooming services at regular intervals, carefully straightening his shirt collar or lightly brushing his closely shaved head with her fingers.

Elizabeth turned her attention to Marie, now beaming and chatting to Gustaf. He was holding forth from his superior vantage point, making sage comments and observations to his sister.

" Marie, Haiti is a very big country. It's much bigger than St. Georges. See those trees. They're mango trees."

The tap-tap pulled in at a gas station, the last one before the rural route. A brightly colored vehicle about the size of a bus pulled in on the other side. It was filled with about three times the number of people in the tap-tap, and was on some kind of a church outing. A man holding a hymn book stood in the aisle leading the party in a gospel melody. The singing undulated from the bus to the tap-tap, where it gathered a responsive humming that slowly gave way to a full-throated reply from a group of tap-tap passengers. Elizabeth felt a surge of life start to quicken within her. If these people in this crowded, uncomfortable, little truck could transcend their physical hardship to reach out and joyously experience life's little pleasures, so too could she. She looked at Bernard, who nodded with pride, acknowledging her admiration.

The crowded streets gave way to green countryside and the tap-tap picked up speed. It hurtled down the pock-marked road as if in frenzied exuberance at its escape from the stranglehold of the city. It was a death defying ride as drivers jockeyed for position, maneuvering through the narrow isthmuses of asphalt, at the edges of the huge craters burned into the roads during times of civil unrest and never repaired. A cry of *Chofè rete la!* or *Ale chofè!* "Stop, chaffeur!" or "Go, chaffeur!" temporarily brought the driver to his senses as he stopped along the roadside to allow someone off or on. If the human voice was unable to prevail, a loud "tap-tap" sound was struck on the sides of his vehicle with a stone or stick, reminding him of his primary purpose to deliver people and goods.

Wooden houses – some brightly colored, others not – were interspersed with thatched-roofed wattle homes, and cacti hedgerows enveloped the small holdings.

At one stop, a young boy ran out to greet the tap-tap, shameless in his nakedness, until he glimpsed Elizabeth amongst his kin. He quickly covered his crotch with his hands, while his face registered gleeful shock. She averted her gaze and helped a women unload her sacks of rice over the side of the tap-tap.

Finally, the tap-tap came to its turn-around rest site and disgorged its remaining passengers. Milot, a delightfully picturesque town, sat nestled in the foothills, with neatly arranged streets paved with brick. The black-domed Catholic church held a dominant position, overlooking the town and its parishioners. As Milot was the gateway to Sans Souci and the great mountain-top fortress, La Citadelle, tourism had spread a benevolent air of comfort, if not prosperity, over the quiet town.

"Let's have some lunch," Bernard suggested. "And then we will search for Aunty."

He chose a small guesthouse where he knew the food

would not upset Elizabeth's foreign stomach, and which had the added advantage of a telephone. He had been to Milot many times with tourists and knew a number of the inhabitants. But he had never heard of the family name Louima. He made some phone calls and sent the word out that they were searching for a Françoise Louima.

Lunch was a delectable avocado salad with lime dressing, followed by a hearty bean soup served with thick crusty bread. As Elizabeth savored her rich Haitian coffee, a lanky unkempt man came in and greeted Bernard with the familiarity of a comrade. He had a broad, crooked-toothed smile, and wore a black tank top, faded charcoal jeans, and ill-fitting tennis shoes. He reported that the woman they sought no longer lived in the town, but had moved up the mountainside and was now living with a man called Henri Jean-Baptiste.

Bernard greeted the news with some concern. He explained to Elizabeth that conditions on the mountainside were often extremely basic, with many of the children never getting a chance to go to school. Elizabeth asked where the nearest school was, and Bernard promised he would point it out to her on the way up the mountain.

They agreed to rendezvous with Bernard's friend, Jean, at Sans Souci in one hour. He would be waiting for them with horses to assist them up the steep paved road that led to La Citadelle. Françoise lived halfway up the route.

The horses turned out to be tough-footed ponies, and gaunt like their owner. A certain keenness in their eyes suggested they were up to the task. At first Elizabeth was reluctant to mount her pony, preferring to let it carry her backpack while she led it on foot. The children were eager cowboys, though, and showed no fear as they grasped the front of their saddles. After about one and a half kilometers of what felt like a vertical incline, Elizabeth mounted her pony to take a rest.

The route was edged with luxuriant growth, skirted by small holdings at regular intervals, with coffee beans spread out to dry on the sun-baked bricks. Children waved from the shadows of their yards.

Elizabeth looked at her watch. It was two in the afternoon.

A cheerful girl of about thirteen came out to greet them and ask if they needed juice. Elizabeth asked if they might have some whole fruit instead. The girl ran on ahead to a house, returning completely out of breath with an armful of ripe oranges.

They came to a stream about three kilometers up the slope, where the ponies made a welcome stop at their watering hole. Jean pointed to a house through the trees on the opposite side of the stream. That was where Françoise lived, he said, and pointed to a small footpath that would take them there. He asked if they wanted him to wait there with the horses in case they needed to return to the town that evening. Elizabeth declined, having decided to walk back down the slope if the quest was in vain.

As they emerged from the trees, the house came into view. It sat squat and sturdy, nestled into a clearing, which was chiseled with a patchwork of cultivation. The roof was traditional thatch, but the walls were constructed with a more modern wood frame. A roofed latrine could be seen in the back.

"It looks not too bad," Bernard remarked.

A goat was tethered in the yard, and a small flock of guinea fowl scattered as they approached. A tall, handsome, barefooted women in her late twenties came out to greet them. She wore a red cotton dress and carried an infant in her arms.

"Salut," she said. *Ou met vini.* "You have come."

She invited them into her home and asked them to be seated on the goat-skin chairs which she had set out for their use. The house was dark, but cool and airy. It was simply furnished, clean and in good order. She had been expecting them.

She went to an inner room and came back bearing a letter, which she gave to Elizabeth. "Josef leave this for Elizabeth," she said in faltering English.

She then went and embraced the two children, and appeared to be looking for signs of her sister as she ran her fingers over their features. She seemed to find a resemblance in Marie's soft eyes and Gustaf's tall lean frame. The conversation was awkward at first as the two women communicated through Bernard, but he proved adept in his role as medium, reconstructing the messages with flair and ease.

They had many things to talk about: Claire's illness, which she had concealed from her family until Aunt Jessie had written to say she was dying; life on St. Georges, which was a source of great interest to Françoise; and the children's schooling and well-being, which was Elizabeth's primary concern.

Françoise said that she had a hard-working man who would see that the children did not want for food and shelter, and that she would love and care for them as her own. But, she confessed, the cost of schooling was a luxury that they may not be able to afford. Elizabeth said that she would talk to the nuns at the mission school and see what arrangements she could make. She would go down the mountain tomorrow and return to Françoise with news later in the day.

As dusk descended on the homestead, a broad-shouldered bull of a man appeared, filling the doorway. He nodded to his wife, then inspected the visitors and extended his hand to Elizabeth in quiet welcome. His size was intimidating, but his demeanor gentle. Yet she could see a wariness in Marie's eyes and in Gustaf's, a fearful respect. The evening meal helped break down some of the reserve, and Bernard concentrated on striking up a conversation with Henri. Elizabeth decided that Bernard was worth his weight in gold and she would have been lost without him.

After the meal, Elizabeth helped Françoise with the cleanup, leaving Bernard to continue his efforts with the quiet Henri. Françoise showed Elizabeth the small room that Marie and Gustaf would share and which would also serve as her room while she was there. Bernard would sleep on a hammock on the porch.

Later that night when the children were asleep, Elizabeth took a flashlight from her backpack and opened the envelope that Françoise had given her upon arrival.

Chère Elizabeth, you are well I hope. The woman Françoise she is good. Her man he is good aussi. The children will be okay. Do not worry. I like to see you when you are in Haiti. I like it very much.

My heart has much to say, but my head not let me.
God Bless You
Josef

CHAPTER 15

Early next morning, Elizabeth walked down the mountainside with Bernard, leaving the children to explore their new surroundings on their own. The mountain air was cool and freshened by a damp breeze still heavy with the morning dew. She strode out with keen intent, her mind focused on the education of the children. She was trying to sweep a wave of apprehension back into the shadows where it had lurked all night.

"Slow down," Bernard cautioned. "I have walked this path many times, you must go slowly or your muscles will get sore."

"Okay," she sighed, gearing down physically, while her mental pace continued at a gallop, dangerously close to bolting out of control. Halfway down Bernard put up his hand to indicate a rest and they both sat down under the shade of a large tree.

"It's so far to the school," she said at last. "How will the children manage?"

"Listen," he said. "People walk long distances here all the time. It's not unusual." But his assurance sounded hollow. "Perhaps they could stay in town during the week and go home at the weekends," he offered. "The sisters at the mission school will be able to help."

They continued their trek in silence. Elizabeth slowly reined in her racing thoughts and felt somewhat reassured knowing that the school was run by a group of Canadian sisters.

~~~

The school was a cheery, white-faced wooden structure with a simple cross on the gable end. Elizabeth went inside. She was relieved to find that, though French was the mother tongue, the sister that greeted her – Sister Thérèse – was also fluent in English. Finding a soul with whom she could easily converse was a great relief. The sister ushered Elizabeth and Bernard into an office where they could sit and talk. They discussed curriculum and standards and where the children might best fit in. The cost of schooling was not high – ten dollars U.S. a month plus books – but still an amount unaffordable to most peasant farmers. Elizabeth left a deposit that would cover the first six months, with an agreement to review the situation at that time.

The discussion then turned to the possibility of room and board for the children during the week. The sister had a list of homes she thought might be suitable. Bernard recognized one of the names on the list, and offered to take Elizabeth to meet them.

Sister Thérèse asked Elizabeth about her plans when her contract was finished and if she would consider coming to Haiti.

"First of all, I need to go home for a long break. I couldn't even get my head around that question right now," she admitted.

Sister Thérèse smiled at her, and quietly handed her a slip of paper with her name and the address of the school. "Just so you know where to find us."

~~~

They arrived back at the farm to be greeted by a pair of dirty, tired, but happy, children. They had spent most of the morning climbing trees – a scarce resource in St. Georges. They had teamed up with four neighbor children who had come to check them out. In the afternoon, they had been pressed into service and sent off with plastic pails to pick coffee beans. They now proudly displayed the fruits of their gathering to Elizabeth, and regaled her with stories of their exploits. The other four children added details as necessary. The conversation rattled back and forth from English to Creole, with some French thrown in by Elizabeth as she attempted to communicate with the newfound friends.

"However bad my French is now," she joked to Bernard, "it will be a total mish-mash if I stay here much longer." She gave Françoise the flour, rice, and macaroni that she had bought in the town and jointly toted up the mountainside with Bernard.

Mèsi anpil! "Thank you very much!" Françoise said with delight.

Supper was quiet, Henri's huge frame cast a silent aura over the gathering. But tonight the silence was one of ease. Marie and Gustaf looked at the big man in awe as he ladled them out second helpings of goat stew and rice.

Later that night Elizabeth broached the subject of her leaving. Gustaf seemed ready, but Marie looked up at her with wet black eyes, at last Elizabeth relented. "Perhaps I can stay for another day or two."

When the children were asleep, she went out to the porch to take in some fresh air and found Bernard sitting there, alone. She took out her ticket; her flight to Canada left from Port au Prince in three days' time.

"Bernard, if I stay here two more days, what are my chances of visiting Gonaives en route to Port au Prince and still making my flight?" she asked.

He shook his head. "You would have to leave day after tomorrow, at the latest, and even that would leave you very little time in Gonaives."

"My problem is, I don't know whether Josef is in Gonaives or Port au Prince. The only address I have for him is in Gonaives."

"Tell me about Josef," he said with a directness that caught her off guard.

"What's there to tell?" she said with uncharacteristic bitterness. "He's my friend, he was deported, life's a bitch!"

But in the quiet stillness of the night, she began to talk about the gentle, faithful, good-humored man she had come to know and had built bridges with across the great divide of race, culture and class, exploring her own heart as she spoke.

"I only know his heart, not his mind, and it is pure – kindly – and radiant," she began, slowly and reflectively. "He is very poor in material things, but rich in spirit and noble in intent. He likes milk in his coffee and sugar in his tea and can coax a fish out of the sea with nothing more than a line, a hook, and a swish of his arm," she added with a flourish.

For a while there was silence, then at last Bernard spoke. "If you were to take a bus to Gonaives, early on Friday morning, you could stay there for the day and catch a plane that evening to Port au Prince. You would then have a day to spend in Port au Prince if you needed it."

She decided to sleep on it and see what tomorrow would bring.

~~~

Sleep was fitful for Elizabeth that night. Wild dreams, induced by the exotic vibrancy of the place, coaxed her out into the wet, rich fields, where she wandered about in search of someone. She came to the stream by the woods, but it had grown monstrous and engorged, its angry waters flushing the red soil into its distended belly. She had to cross it and looked around frantically for a passage. Further upstream she spotted a flash of light, illuminating a wooden bridge. She made her way to the bridge and tentatively placed a hand on the rope-hold that swung between the poles spanning its length at irregular intervals. As she started to cross, the water boiled over the wooden struts, beating her around the ankles, and driving her forward. The bridge tipped sideways as a torrent of water broke over the edge, sweeping her into its churning fury. Clay-saturated water stifled her cries as she sank beneath the fomenting waters. At the point of blankness, her arm was grasped and pulled towards the bank. She was heaved out of the water into a hard embrace that softened as her safety was assured. The night was an inpenetrable pitch black, and only the familiar contours and smell of the warm body that cradled her limp one, spoke of the identity of her rescuer.

~ ~ ~

"Would you like to see La Citadelle?" Bernard asked the following morning. "It was built by King Henri Christophe in the early eighteen hundreds, as a fortress retreat in case the French ever returned. It's just three more kilometers to the top from here."

C'est une mervielle, "It's a marvel," Françoise enthused.

Even Henri lit up at the mention of the Citadelle. He

announced that he would take them there if they wished, adding some disparaging remarks in the direction of Bernard in jestful insinuation of his lack of knowledge on the subject. He then proceeded to instruct the children on the importance of the fortress to the history of Haiti.

"Sounds like we've got an expedition," Elizabeth agreed. Bernard hurled a few insults in Henri's direction, but it was clear from the expressions on both men's faces that neither intended to give offense. Françoise prepared food for when they got to the top. But she would stay home with the baby.

Elizabeth wondered about the lot of Françoise, and of Haitian women in general. Serial monogamous relationships seemed common amongst the women, while the men indulged in a number of relationships concurrently, often prompted by their shifting living and work patterns. She wondered how many other children Henri had fathered. He looked like he was in his forties, which made it somewhat unlikely that baby Michelle was his first offspring. She wondered about Josef, who she figured was in his mid-thirties. What did his past hold?

~~~

Henri led the expedition. He took slow deliberate strides and kept a watchful eye on his entourage, easing up when the group flagged or moaned and complained. He stopped at one point and scooped Marie up in his powerful arms, seating her on his shoulders. She gave a haughty little smirk at Gustaf, who stuck his chest out in disdain and quickened his pace to keep abreast of Henri.

It was only in the last kilometer that the fortress became visible, looming large on the skyline as they rounded one more bend.

"My God, it's massive!" Elizabeth gasped. She peered up at the huge structure, built from hand-cut limestone blocks, and the sweat and blood of twenty thousand "freed slaves", forced into labor. The mega-project took twenty years and was never quite completed. The megalomaniac, Henri Christophe, who presided over the project in despotic style, had suffered a stroke before its completion. Fearing capture from his rival Dessaulines, he had committed suicide with a silver bullet, in one last grandiose act.

A large round tower marked its approach. The road curved around its buttressed foundations and swept upwards to its wide main frontage and entrance port. The structure lured them on like a magnet and tired foot-draggers sprang forward for the final ascent. Once there, they sat down at the base of the fortress and surveyed the panoramic view of mountains, spellbound by the grandeur and splendor of it all.

From her vantage point, Elizabeth spotted a solitary figure on an opposing mountain peak. What urge, she wondered, had lured that human soul up into the mountain tops, far, far from any human dwelling?

They ate their lunch, and then Henri stretched out on a sloping piece of grassed terrace and promptly went to sleep. Elizabeth looked at Bernard, shrugging her shoulders.

Kou mwen chita, mwen gen domi, he said and laughed. Then he translated the Creole proverb in English: "When I sit down, I fall asleep."

"When in Rome, do as the Romans do," she answered, and they all stretched out on the grass and closed their eyes.

Of course, Marie and Gustaf giggled fitfully for the first ten minutes, but they too, eventually fell under the spell of midday heat and satiated stomachs.

Thirty minutes later, Elizabeth was awakened by a gentle squeeze on the shoulder and a "Bonsoir". All four of her comrades were standing, ready for the grand tour. Henri extended his hand to help her to her feet. "Merci," she said, accepting his help graciously. He smiled expansively and the twinkle in his eye suggested to her that they were in for the complete tour.

Henri started his dissertation in French, but soon lapsed into Creole, saying that it was only fair that he gave Bernard something to do to keep him occupied. They walked the ramparts, surveying the stockpile of cannons and unused cannon balls, some cast in iron and a few in bronze. Some of the cannons had their own unique stories, and Henri knew them all. He showed them the dungeons, the kitchens, the water catchment tanks. There was evidence of restoration work, which had recently been carried out with help from a U.N.E.S.C.O. World Heritage Site fund. They toured the museum, and every little plaque was brought to life by Henri's vivid description. From the top of the battlements they could see the sweep of mountains all the way to Cap Hatien and the sea.

Finally, they sat around a large wooden table in what would have been the officers' eating quarters, and Henri looked at Elizabeth and said, "Now tell me about Canada, Elizabeth." He folded his arms, indicating that it was now her turn and that he was finished.

She happily wove a tapestry of images worthy of her homeland, which she loved so much. "What a wonderful world we live in," she said in closure, and they all agreed.

The adults made their way down the mountainside in silence, each in private contemplation. The children ran on ahead laughing and jostling with each other, but ran out of steam about two thirds of the way from the house. Marie put her arms out to Henri, who willingly put her back on her perch. They stopped at one of the wayside homes to buy some fresh oranges, as requested by Françoise. Henri coaxed the woman into throwing a seed-strung bracelet into the deal.

When they arrived at the house, Françoise came out to greet them and Henri presented her with both the bracelet and the oranges. He deftly swung the sleeping Marie off his shoulders and gently placed her onto the hammock.

Elizabeth looked at Bernard. "I think it's time for us to go. We will leave first thing tomorrow morning," she said. Bernard smiled in agreement.

CHAPTER 16

The ladder shuddered between its loosely held supports. The man standing on its second last rung threw the rope up to Josef, who then looped it around a pipe on the scaffold and hauled the bucket of plaster up to the third storey. He dumped the plaster onto a wooden palate, returned the bucket to the man below, then went back to his work. This procedure would be repeated each time he needed more material.

He was working alone on a small window lintel, which jutted out from the main structure. He had landed the job two days ago, after an ill-fated plasterer had lost his footing on the open scaffolding and had fallen three storeys and broken his hip. The man's misfortune had provided Josef with his first chance of work since returning to Haiti three weeks ago.

He disliked Port au Prince. It symbolized all that seemed to be strangling and terrorizing his country. The mansions on the mountainsides, which he could see all too plainly from his third-storey work site, stood aloof and unconcerned, high enough to breathe fresh air, while those that built, serviced and fed them toiled in the stench-filled air of the congested lower slopes. Josef wasn't a politician; indeed, he had little faith in politics, having lived long enough to see that changing the faces of the people in power made little changes in the lives of the masses. What did it matter who was in power? Did it mean that he would have to work any less hard or earn more money? The billboards, with their promises of progress, lured people to the cities for jobs that were not there. Yet they kept coming. And amongst them the thugs, who, seeing no government and no security, terrorized the meek and made deals with the compromising. What saddened him the most was that he could see no way out of the misery.

~~~

He had arrived back in Gonaives to find his parents and relatives in much the same state as when he had left. His brother, Jean, worked six days a week at a local store to feed and clothe his family. But still, it was the money Josef had sent that was paying for the education of Jean's eldest daughter. His mother had spent nothing of what he had sent on herself, but had passed it all on to the other children and grandchildren as she saw the need. When he asked her why she had not bought a new mattress for her bed as he had hoped, she had laughed and told him she liked the old mattress fine.

He had spent a week with them. There had been much excitement and rejoicing at his return, and a string of cousins had come by to hear of life and prospects in St. Georges and perhaps share in his good fortune. When was he going back? Could he find a job for them? Could he lend them some money? The intricacies of work permits seemed unimportant to them.

There had been a party one night, with music and dancing, and beer for those who were drinking. There was a swaying mass of bodies under the stars, intoxicated by the drumming and the alcohol. Josef's natural reticence was overcome by the beat of the drum, which he loved, and the one beer that he had indulged in at the insistence of his cousin who had bought it cheap.

One man had brought his eighteen-year-old daughter over to him, wondering if he might take her back with him to cook, wash, iron, and perhaps please him in other ways. The man had left her with him while he went in search of more drink, and the girl had started to move to the drumbeat inviting him to join her. The girl was pleasing to look at: her body was sculpted in soft round curves and her teeth flashed white.

Josef laughed and started to dance with her, self-consciously at first. But soon, he gave himself over to the rhythm of the drum and closed his eyes in brief respite. She moved closer to him. He felt her breasts sweep lightly across his chest, felt the warmth of her breath on his cheeks. When he looked into her eyes in search of meaning and intent, he found a vacancy that shocked him. What had been erotic a moment ago was now mechanical and repulsive to him. He retreated.

That night he was haunted by those eyes, so young and yet devoid of dreams or aspirations. He wondered to what depths of despair his country was plunging towards, that one so young could be so old, and that a father would willingly send his child into servitude.

The next day he set off for Port au Prince, where he had heard a lot of new construction was in progress. Before leaving, he spent time with his mother. He told her he didn't know if it would be possible for him to return to St. Georges, but that he had friends there who might be able to help him get a work permit. He told her of Claire and her children, and of the white woman, Elizabeth, who was his friend.

She had listened without interrupting him. *Mwen fini vie. Mwen pa bezwen an yin anko. Selman mwen vle pou ka kontan,* "I am at the end of my life. I have need of little. My one desire is for your happiness," she had said as she kissed him goodbye.

He'd thought about her words on the way to Port au Prince and wondered what was it that would make him happy. Sitting on a sack of flour in the middle of the tap-tap, he pushed back thoughts and desires he didn't even dare dream about as he mulled over his situation. He downgraded his aspirations to goals he thought might be attainable. Then he became angry at his mother for having tempted him with what seemed beyond his reach.

~~~

Plis siman! "More cement!" Josef shouted, looking over the edge.

A young man, no more than a boy of sixteen, started to climb the ladder with the bucket of plaster. *Mwen vini,* "I'm coming," he said, hauling the bucket awkwardly as he climbed. He flashed a smile at Josef, his eyes bright, glad of the work.

In them, Josef saw a reflection of himself, twenty years earlier. He wondered what he had accomplished in all those years. He remembered a brief period of happiness in his early twenties, almost delirious in its sweetness and ecstasy. Theoline: petite, slender, and elegant, her soft skin three shades lighter than his own. She sat with her basket of fruit every morning on the corner of Rue Goulet. Every morning he would walk an extra kilometer just to pass her stall, and smile and greet her. Every evening he would return by the same route, hoping she would not yet be gone, so that he could stop and buy her oranges or mangos. Eventually, he was feeding all the neighbors' children with fruit, and his aunt, with whom he was living, upbraided him for squandering his money. Fortunately, Theoline had fallen for him just as his list of people for whom he could buy fruit had been exhausted. One evening, she was waiting there for him. Everybody else had left. Her eyes, full of expectation, betrayed her fear and vulnerability. He had fallen madly in love with her then, and courted her with all the earnestness and passion in his intoxicated heart and soul.

Her mother, Jacqueline, had been a maid at one or other of the large homes built on the higher slopes. Theoline had been the result of a brief affair with a mulatto man that Jacqueline had worked for when she first came to Port au Prince from the countryside. He was married, and her pregnancy put an end to the affair after his wife made some quick deductions. But he did build her a small, sturdy home on the mountainside on a small piece of property to which he had title. Its proximity to wealthy homes meant she had never been out of work. Theoline's brothers were the offspring of a periodic but stable relationship, interspersed by long absences. This had the benefit of reducing the number of children, but also left Jacqueline in a fitful pendulum between poverty and comfort. She took life as it was dished out to her, and was happy with her children and content with her lot. She had taken an instant liking to Josef, and very soon he was a regular at their supper table.

The grinding days at the building site evaporated at the sight of Theoline, and Sundays were bliss: all morning at church, where his spirit soared, and all afternoon with her, when every fibre of his being became alive and glowed warm and tender.

After six months, they decided to get married. He was twenty-two and she was eighteen. Jacqueline gave her blessing, but Josef's mother was not happy and tried to dissuade him: he would never rise out of poverty if he took on dependents this early in life. But he was determined and too happy to see any possible downfalls to the union.

And so they were wed. He built an extra room onto Jacqueline's house and moved in with them. Josef was happy to share what he had with the whole household. Everybody got along well, but there never seemed to be anything extra beyond their basic needs.

When Theoline became pregnant, Josef was ecstatic...

"Atansyon! Atansyon!" one of the men shouted at the base of the ladder. He lunged forward in an attempt to stabilize it. The young man on it scrambled frantically, trying to rebalance his load and gain control of the tottering ladder. Josef swung down the scaffold in a desperate attempt to reach the boy. He caught his arm for a brief instant – just long enough to turn a headlong plunge into a vertical drop. It probably saved the boy's life; but he nevertheless sustained a broken ankle, and Josef sustained some torn shoulder muscles. They headed off to the hospital together to get patched up.

Thirty minutes later, Elizabeth arrived on the site. It had taken quite a bit of detective work, but she had found people to be very helpful and quite intrigued at the object of her search. Her final sleuthing had been aided by an enthusiastic taxi driver. He knew all the construction sites in Port au Prince, and he honked and barged his way through intersections, ran his car up on pavements to access awkward sites, and jumped out of his vehicle waving a photo of Josef and shouting his name up and down the ranks of workers. This was their fourth site, and he assured her he had a really good feeling about it.

Yes! This was the one! But Elizabeth's initial exhilaration was followed by disappointment upon learning that Josef had left less than an hour ago to go to the hospital. She debated whether she should go to the hospital or wait there. She decided to stay put, having been assured that Josef was not hurt badly. He would most likely leave the boy at the hospital and return immediately to the work site.

She asked the taxi driver to return in exactly one hour to take her to the airport. He left with an air of self-satisfaction, assuring her he would not fail her.

She sat on an unopened sack of dry cement under the

watchful gaze of the workers. They filed past her as they returned to work, some smiling, some nodding, and some staring hard without betraying any emotion or intent. She had found this stare the most discomforting, and it was one she had noticed at other times during her visit.

As the men resumed their work, she caught snatches of conversations; she knew enough Creole words to conclude that she was the main topic of conversation. Words such as *blanche* white woman, *etranje* foreigner, *Josef* and *renmen* (which could mean girlfriend, love, like, or, simply, be fond of, depending on context) were being bandied about.

She watched the men as they toiled in the heat and air tainted with leaded gasoline fumes, using simple tools and outdated, hazardous equipment. She thought about the sprawling shanties and appalling living conditions she had witnessed during her wild taxi ride, and wondered how many of these men returned to such conditions at night. Josef's home outside Gonaives had been relatively comfortable compared to these and even that had been outside the realm of her experience. She tried to imagine herself living that way, cooking without electricity, hauling water, and using an outside latrine. The latter sent a particularly odious shudder down her spine.

She started to wonder what on earth it was that seemed to connect her to Josef, began to feel awkward if not outright stupid.

She looked at her watch. It was four thirty. The taxi would be here in another fifteen minutes.

As she lifted her head she saw a medium-framed man approaching. He wore blue jeans and a yellow tank top, and looked no different from the dozen or so other workers on the site. But when he saw her, he stopped dead in his tracks, one hand on his hip. His face, at first quizzical, rapidly transformed into a picture of sheer joy. She stood up. She felt a surge of blood in her cheeks and she started to feel unsteady on her feet. But his eyes were constant and focused completely on her, steadying her, and at the same time, continuing to unnerve her. When at last he was close enough to extend his hand to her, she ignored it, and instead wrapped him in a warm embrace. He held her with his left arm. His right arm hung loosely by his side.

"How are you? Are you hurt?" she asked, releasing him. She examined the injury, cautiously rubbing his shoulder and forearm.

"It's okay," he said and gently lowered her arm, slipping his hand in hers and drawing her down to sit on the cement sacks. "I am very happy to see you. Tell me about you and the children."

She told tell him of their journey. Of how she felt Henri would be a good father to them, and how it would probably be okay for them in their new home. She told him that she had arranged for them to attend school, but that she would come back and check on them in September.

"And check on me, too?" he said with a grin.

"Peut-être," she said nonchalantly. "Tell me, my friend, are you coming back to St. Georges, if you can?"

"Peut-être," he said, and she smiled.

They exchanged addresses just as the taxi appeared, honking its horn and bumping its way over the pot-holed site. Josef opened the door for her, then asked the driver to wait a moment. He quickly went and had a word with the foreman. He returned and got in beside her.

"I come to the airplane with you," he said.

He put his good arm lightly around her shoulder. She rested her head against him. They never uttered a word all the way to the airport.

CHAPTER 17

"Hi, Mom! How was Haiti?" Michelle threw her arms around Elizabeth.

"Fascinating! It's a long story, we'll talk about it later. How are you?"

"Great, I've got a job at the Y for the summer, so we'll see lots of each other. Mom, this is Sam, he's going to give us a ride home."

Elizabeth eyed the earnest-looking young man in his early twenties. He had a slender, medium frame, with Mediterranean features and olive skin. His dark brown hair was pulled neatly into a ponytail.

"Nice to meet you, Sam. Thanks for coming to collect me."

"My pleasure, Mrs. Bourke," he said a little awkwardly, extending his hand to her.

"Gosh, I can hardly believe I'm back," she said.

Elizabeth looked around and drank in the familiar atmosphere. The Winnipeg airport was international in the mix of peoples filtering through its doors, yet lacked the harried turmoil characteristic of so many airports. A major doorway to northern Manitoba and the Arctic, there was a number of Canada's aboriginal people making their way to or from their vastly scattered settlements. She caught the familiar intonations of the native accents, interspersed with some Cree and Inuktitut. It was pleasant to her ears, and she felt a warm wave flow through her body.

"Where are your bags, Mrs. Bourke?" Sam asked.

"It's just this backpack," Elizabeth replied, as she slipped it to the ground from her shoulders.

"Here, let me take it," he said. "That's it?"

"That's it. I needed to travel light in Haiti. And in any case, it's time I bought myself some new clothes."

"Great, you can take me shopping with you, I need some new clothes too," Michelle said. Elizabeth smiled and slipped her arm around her daughter's waist. The two women went through the automatic doors, with Sam quietly bringing up the rear.

Sam's little Chevette scooted along the well-maintained roads and quietly made its way through the four-way stop signs in an orderly fashion. Sam uttered a few low key tut-tuts as he maneuvered around the few remaining potholes that had yet to be repaired after the spring thaw.

"Consider yourself lucky, Sam," Elizabeth said. "If this was Haiti, that pothole would have been ten times the size and you'd probably have been rear-ended at the last intersection, or at the very least honked at. He who hesitates in Haiti is definitely lost. On the other hand, you'd do just fine in St. Georges, as long as you didn't mind driving on the wrong side of the road!"

"Did you take any photos?" asked Michelle.

"A few, but the ones that are developed are of St. Georges." They pulled into the parking lot behind Michelle's apartment building and Sam brought the backpack up. Michelle fussed with her keys as she made her way through two sets of doors before reaching her own apartment.

"Ready for a cup of tea, Mom?"

"You bet!"

Sam headed for the door, but Michelle prevailed on him to stay and have a cup of tea.

"I want you to see Mom's photos," she said.

They looked at the photos over a cup of tea. There were ones of the Christmas party at the Governor's, ones of school graduation, and a variety of shots taken by the house. There was one of Josef, bent over with a machete in his hand as he cleared some scrub.

"That's Josef," Michelle said to Sam. "He's a friend of Mom's. Look! here are the shots of me diving," Michelle said, excitedly. "That's a good one, Mom." She said referred to an underwater shot Elizabeth had taken just below the surface.

"Who is this?" Sam asked. He pointed to a photo of a smiling Michelle holding up a certificate in one hand, while being embraced and kissed on the cheek by an enthusiastic Stanley.

"One of the dive masters," Michelle stated casually, and without further comment, she flipped through the rest of the photos.

Sam looked at his watch. "I have to go," he said.

"Nice meeting you, Sam, and thanks again for coming to the airport," Elizabeth said.

Sam smiled warmly and just a little self-consciously.

Michelle got up and walked him to the door. "See you tomorrow," she said, and she put her finger to her lips and then placed it on his.

"Well, what do you think?" She closed the door and swung around to face her mother.

"Was I supposed to be making an assessment?" Elizabeth replied mockingly. "He seems nice. What does he do?"

"He is doing a PhD in physics."

"He wouldn't be Albert Einstein, *the dork!* by any chance, would he?"

Michelle laughed. "You've a memory like an elephant, Mom. Yes, but he's improved a lot since he met me."

"I can see that. Is he always that quiet?"

"No, but he was really uptight about meeting you. His parents are giving him a hard time about going out with a *shiksa*. They're very Jewish."

"Hmmm, let's take it one day at a time, shall we," Elizabeth said reflectively. "Most of my notions of social and religious boundaries have been irreparably damaged. But, I can see how strong they are and how tenaciously they are held onto by many. I take it this is serious, so I will give him a thorough vetting next chance I get."

"I've invited him for supper tomorrow night."

"Looks like I got home just in time."

"Yep," Michelle said. "We need an ally. Sally's coming and she's bringing dessert. She says she can't wait to see you."

"Great, I'm looking forward to that. Now, I think it's time for my first indulgence — a long, hot bath."

Elizabeth undressed slowly, as she watched the steam rise out of the bath enticingly. It had been dry for months in St. Georges and she had been forced to conserve water carefully, confining herself to very short showers. This was going to be pure bliss.

She took off her blouse and pressed it against her face. It still had the scents of Haiti clinging to it. On the surface was a layer of Port au Prince smog. Slightly deeper was the aroma of oranges and mangos — an aroma that had penetrated the taxi from the shopping bag of its previous client. And when she inhaled deeply, she could smell the musk of skin — not her own, but that left from the arm that had enfolded her on her way to the airport.

She hesitated slightly before discarding the blouse in the laundry basket, and then stepped into the bath and gave herself up to the liquid balm. She thought of the daughter who had become a woman in her absence and, it appeared, was forging an identity that may very well be linked to the quiet, intense man named Sam. She submerged herself fully in the water, along with all thoughts of her own complicated attachments.

~~~

She slept in the next morning until ten and when she got up, found a note on the table from Michelle: "Gone shopping, breakfast is in the fridge." She opened the fridge door and was surprised to find a large blueberry bagel, sitting on a plate with a lump of cream cheese beside it, covered in plastic wrap. There was a pot of hot coffee, patiently waiting on the stove, and the table was neatly laid for one.

Elizabeth sat and had breakfast, surveying the living/dining area of the apartment as she ate. It seemed bigger and tidier than she remembered. It probably just looked bigger because she had become accustomed to smaller houses; but, yes, it was definitely tidier. There was less clutter, and Michelle had discarded a lot of the posters and calendar prints, replacing them with a large batik wall-hanging depicting atomic and subatomic particles in a waltz of color and contour. Some of her favorite photos had been framed and formed a geometric design on another wall. One deliberately errant photo was cocked brazenly out of kilter with the words "dare to be out of step" emblazoned on it.

Elizabeth examined the other photos closely. There was a family photo taken on Michelle's sixteenth birthday, the last one taken while Matt was alive. There was one of Michelle on her horse, Jimmy, clearing a sizeable jump. And there were two placed side by side: one of Matt and one of Sam. Oh dear, Elizabeth thought, this really is serious, and she wondered how this relationship had blossomed without her picking it up in Michelle's correspondence.

Michelle breezed in at about eleven, laden down with shopping bags. "I'm going all out with this one," she said, showing Elizabeth the avocado, planned as a starter, and the chicken breasts she would use for a stir-fry.

"Who are you trying to impress, me or Sam?"

"You, actually," she replied. "He's been living on his own longer than I have and is a pretty good cook. The real reason is I have to get some practice in before his parents come to town in August. I'm counting on you to have me up to speed by then. This is just to give you an idea of what you're up against."

"How come you never mentioned Sam in your letters?"

"Well, as you know, our relationship started off on an antagonistic note. But then it kinda grew into mutual respect. We saw a lot of each other during the year, because of my lab load. He helped me with some extra tutorials just before my last exam — which I aced, by the way. We've been seeing each other since the end of term, and everything's been just great. Since you haven't written much since the end of May, there wasn't anything to tell. Besides, I knew you would get plenty of chance to meet him once you got home."

"I have been preoccupied," Elizabeth confessed. "But you have my full attention now."

CHAPTER 18

The avocado was sliced and neatly arranged in a pinwheel pattern on a bed of lettuce. Fresh lime-juice vinaigrette had been drizzled over the avocado flesh, with slivers of lime and tomato to decorate. The ensemble was displayed in a hand-carved, two-tone wooden bowl, which Elizabeth had bought in Cap Hatien.

Elizabeth mused over the humble quarters where she had squatted on the floor with the bowl's creator as they haggled over the price. Elizabeth's slow pondering over the asking price had been interpreted as reluctance, when in fact it had been chiefly the result of the mathematical somersaults she had wrestled with, to convert gourdes to Hatian dollars and then to U.S. dollars. Each time she shook her head in confusion, he lowered his price, explaining to her that she was his first customer of the day, so he had to sell to her, but he couldn't give his bowl away. Just as he had come to his final offer, she had gotten the hang of the conversion rate and they came to an agreement. She had certainly paid more for it than a Haitian national would have, but for a tourist she had more than held her own.

"Do you want me to put napkins out?" she asked Michelle, who was busy preparing the chicken in the kitchen.

"Yes, yes, whatever," came the harried reply. "Mom, come into the kitchen quick, I need your help!"

A charred smell assailed Elizabeth as she entered the kitchen. The rice had boiled over and the starchy water was sputtering and steaming on a red-hot element. Elizabeth lurched forward and quickly removed it from the hot element. Michelle's attention was focused on the chicken breasts, which were skinless, fat free, and sticking stubbornly to the bottom of the frying pan.

"Time out," Elizabeth suggested as she turned off the ring. "Okay, no need to panic, just slow the game down. You're going to have to put some butter in with those chicken breasts and just remember to turn the rice down once it comes to a boil."

"You take over the rice, Mum, and I'll beat the chicken into submission. Just don't leave me."

Elizabeth laughed. A few minutes later, everything was under control again. Shortly thereafter, Sam arrived, clad in khaki cotton pants and a black shirt. He handed Elizabeth a box of chocolates. "How's she doing?" he asked, as if referring to a patient.

"I think she'll make it," Elizabeth laughed. "Thanks for the chocolates."

"Suck up," Michelle accused as she emerged from the kitchen. Examining him approvingly, she added, "I suppose I'd better change my bloodied and spattered T-shirt." She disappeared into her bedroom and left the two of them alone.

"What's your PhD thesis on?" Elizabeth asked.

"I'm working on increasing the efficiency and capacity of solar energy panels."

"Well, lots of sun here in Manitoba to work with."

"Yes, some of my test sites are as far north as Churchill," he said enthusiastically.

"I'm using a series of mirrors to increase the reflected light from the snow…"

As Elizabeth listened, she could see he was genuinely interested in his research, and at least the principle was one she could understand. He was thoughtful enough not to ramble on above her and he answered her questions clearly and concisely.

"Do you like animals?" she asked, changing the subject, and knowing full well that he could forget about any long term relationship with Michelle which excluded them.

"I love animals, but I've never had much contact with them," he admitted. "So I'm a bit awkward around them. Michelle has introduced me to all the animals at the barn and I'm starting to understand the lingo."

"Yes, well at least he's not allergic to them, Mom." Michelle re-appeared in clean jeans and a loose-fitting cheesecloth blouse. "He's a good photographer and he's taken some nice shots of me and Jimmy."

"My mother is allergic to cats and dogs, so we never had any pets growing up, except for a large aquarium of tropical fish," Sam explained.

"Where do your parents live?" asked Elizabeth.

"They used to live in Winnipeg, but they moved back to Toronto two years ago. I decided to stay here, as I was already halfway through my degree. Besides, I like Manitoba," he said, looking at Michelle.

She smiled back at him, and Elizabeth could feel the chemistry that charged between them.

"Knock, knock!" came a voice from the open door. Sally came in carrying a home-baked walnut cake, topped with coffee icing. She quickly set it on the table, then swung round to smother everybody in hugs and kisses. She embraced her old friend with particular vigor, then took her hand and demanded to be told everything.

"Let's eat," Michelle suggested. "Everything's under control in the kitchen right now, but I can't guarantee that it will stay that way while Mom tells her long story."

They all sat down and started on the avocado salad. The conversation flowed easily between life in Manitoba and life in St. Georges. The three women could identify with descriptions and tales of life on the island, and laughed and snorted, adding their own experiences in similar situations.

Sam seemed interested, but not connected, his only experience outside of North America having been a brief trip to Israel. He had told Michelle that his parents had hoped that the trip would emblazon in his heart his Jewish identity, but it had only served to alienate him further from traditions that held little meaning for him. His parents and two older brothers had been galvanized after their trip through the Judean desert and the Jewish settlements in Hebron. But Samuel had seen only barren land and a group of zealots willing to kill or die for it. He was seventeen at the time and his two brothers were studying law. Their fluent arguments had silenced his tongue on the issue, but not his opinions. He had returned to Winnipeg and applied to engineering - much to his father's dismay, whose business interests required accountants and lawyers. Sam was quietly insistent, excelling in math and physics as if to drive home his point. In the end, his father, who secretly admired his tenacity, agreed to support his decision.

It was only when Elizabeth started to tell of the precarious existence of the Haitian community in St. Georges, and of Josef's particular circumstances, that a chord was struck in Sam. "Physically, the earth is one entity," he said, "a small blue ball, hurtling through space, where its boundaries are meaningless. I don't understand the intense attachment and propriety people hold for the pieces they carve up and cling to so tenaciously."

His impassioned interjection took them all by surprise, and Elizabeth wondered just where he was coming from, but Sally understood.

"Yes," Sally said, quoting from the writings of her faith, "The earth is but one country and mankind its citizens."

"My mind, heart, and soul tell me it is so, but my tradition, upbringing, and experience tells me differently," Sam went on.

"That is because we have yet, as a race, to recognize it," Sally said.

"In the meantime, we're busy subdividing the human race into categories and castes. Tell me, Mrs. Bourke," Sam asked. " What are your feelings on inter-faith marriages?"

"Hypothetically, I'm ambivalent. But, if you're asking me how I would feel about my daughter marrying into a Jewish family, then my answer is, it depends! It depends on the level of shared belief between the couple, and the level of accord and unity that exists between the families. Because marriage is meant to unite people, not divide them."

"I agree," Sam said. "And that is our dilemma."

Elizabeth's heart was pounding. This was not her idea of a good start to a nice, uncomplicated rest.

"Don't you think you're jumping the gun a bit?" she asked cautiously.

"Well, not really," Michelle said. "Sam's parents are coming in two weeks and we want you to meet them, knowing that we're seriously contemplating marriage."

"Oh, Michelle, I don't think I'm ready for this," Elizabeth said.

There was an awkward silence, until Sally offered some light news about how various friends of Elizabeth and Matt were doing. Sam and Michelle started to clear the dinner plates and went into the kitchen to make coffee.

"You knew about this, didn't you," Elizabeth said to Sally.

"Well, they've both been coming to a study circle at the Bahá'í Centre, so I'm not surprised."

"And I suppose you're going to tell me that if they were both Bahá'í, their problems would be solved?"

"No, but their study of the faith gives them a neutral and unifying context to view both their spiritual traditions. The Bahá'í faith teaches the unity of religions — that they are all part of God's unfolding plan for humanity."

"Hmm, maybe. We'll see," she said as Sam and Michelle came back with the coffee.

Michelle opened the chocolates and offered her mother one.

"Why is life so complicated? I'm so exhausted at the moment, I have difficulty deciding which chocolate to choose."

"Sorry, Mom." Michelle sat on the sofa and curled up beside her.

The rest of the evening's conversation leveled off to less weighty subjects, such as whether or not the Winnipeg Jets would be sold before the next hockey season. This was the current hot topic in the city and everybody had an opinion. There was a tacit agreement, now that the "big" subject had been aired, that they could all relax and enjoy each other's company. Sam mellowed out and his intensity toned down to a warm glow. He was the sort of guy who only talked when he had something to say; having said it, he quietly let the conversation rattle on around him.

Elizabeth noticed that of the four of them, Michelle was the one most at ease. Elizabeth had never seen her display such quiet assurance. She was obviously very well pleased with her man.

Later that night, when it was just the two of them, Michelle asked once again, "Now what do you think, Mom?"

"I think I've got two weeks to figure that one out. But let's just say he's off to a good start."

CHAPTER 19

The next day, they went on a shopping trip together. Portage Place was full of people. It was a gathering place, not only for shoppers, but also for youth, the elderly, and an assortment of vagrants. Elizabeth found herself watching people with interest and making eye contact with them as she passed.

"What are you doing, Mom? Stop gawking and keep up or we'll never get anything."

Elizabeth spotted two young girls, about ten and eight years old, unaccompanied and unkempt, wandering around the food court. They disappeared into the bathroom and Elizabeth hurried to catch up with Michelle.

They checked out the boutiques, and went in and out of three in a row without any purchases. Elizabeth saw lots of things she liked, but she thought that they were either too expensive, or not really what she wanted. The choice was overwhelming, and after an initial burst of enthusiasm, she quickly became apathetic and a glazed look came over her eyes. Michelle, on the other hand, knew exactly what she wanted, searching methodically. But she couldn't find it. Two hours later, all they had bought between them was some underwear and a pair of shoes.

"Let's have something to eat," Elizabeth suggested.

They made their way to the food court and decided to head for the pizza counter. Out of the corner of her eye, Elizabeth noticed the two young girls sitting at a table sharing some fries. The older one's long black hair fell loosely over her shoulders and across the front of her soiled white T-shirt, partly concealing the graphic of an eagle and "Dakota Tribal Days" inscribed beneath. The younger one had her hair in a single braid behind and wore a slightly cleaner red version of the same T-shirt.

Elizabeth ordered two extra pieces of pizza and went and sat at the table next to them. After about five minutes, she leant back and put her hands on her stomach. "I'm full," she groaned. "Would you girls like some pizza?" she asked, looking across the table to the two young girls.

The older one nodded but avoided eye contact with her. Elizabeth passed her the plate. The younger one smiled, but before Elizabeth could start up a conversation, the older one stood up, grabbing the pizza in one hand and the young girl's hand in the other. "Come on, we have to go," she said, and they quickly made their way to the escalator, devouring pizza as they went.

"What was that all about?" Michelle asked.

"They reminded me of Gustaf and Marie," she answered. "They had the same look in their eyes that Gustaf and Marie had after their mother died. A look of uncertainty, of being unable to count on people or events."

"I thought you said they would be alright, that everything worked out well in Haiti for them."

"Yes, as best I can tell, but I still worry about them, and ...I worry about you," she added. "That perhaps I shouldn't have left when I did, that I should've stayed put, at least until you had finished college."

"Mom, I could just as easily have gone to college out of province. I wouldn't have seen any more of you than I do now. I'm not with Sam because I'm lonely. I'm with him because I love him and because he is my best friend."

"I can see that and I'm really happy for you, but I think you're going to have to take things slowly, especially if you don't want to alienate his parents."

"We will. Now, can you help me find something suitable to wear to a synagogue?"

They headed back into the fray, and before long found themselves deliberating seriously over a cream suit. It had clean, chic lines that made the statement: "I may look like a suit, but I ain't conservative." Michelle tried it on and decided that, though she might never wear the ensemble outside of a church or synagogue, she could put both the skirt and jacket to good use separately. So they bought it.

"Okay, Mom, now that that's out of the way, what are we going to get for you?"

Elizabeth knew she needed to buy some clothes, but wasn't sure what for. Was she looking for things she could wear at cocktail parties, to which she was invited infrequently? Was it for school? Or was it to be deliberately understated — to blur the lines of distinction that might set her apart from friends, or too closely define her position in society? She decided that she needed all three, and opted for a versatile suit to fill the first two functions and light cotton pants and shorts, with some accessories, for the third.

As she sorted through shirts and blouses, her attention was caught by a rack of men's casual shirts. She moved over to the rack and started to examine them more closely. She thought of the few shirts she had seen Josef wear over the past year — always clean, but definitely past their best. On an impulse, she selected two that she thought he would like and that would complement his deep ebony skin. She ignored the raised eyebrow that Michelle arched in her direction and quickly made her way to the cashier.

"I think I've had enough shopping for one day, let's go home," she said.

They made their way out to the back parking lot, where the car she had borrowed from Sally was parked. She got one further glimpse of the two young girls, silently walking down an alley between two large, ugly and decrepit brick buildings. They slipped into a side doorway, and were consumed inside a shell of grimy bricks, and broken, boarded-up windows. Halfway up the facade was a faded cloth banner, *Rooms for Rent*, and out of one open window a beer bottle came hurtling down, shattering in angry jagged pieces on the pavement below. Little Haiti, Elizabeth thought, wondering why she had never really noticed it before.

~~~

"Thanks for the car, Sally," she said as she handed over the keys.

"Come in and have a cup of coffee. Then I'll drive you home."

"You go on, Mom, I'm going to catch a bus downtown. I have to check my schedule at the Y. I think I'm on this Friday. I'll see you later."

Sally poured them both two steaming mugs of coffee. The

aroma was hazelnut, complemented by a fresh baking smell wafting from the oven. "Five minutes more and those cookies will be ready," she said. "Come and look at Ken's latest paintings. He's getting ready for an exhibition."

They went down to the basement and examined a series of acrylic on canvas, characterized by pastel tones and metaphysical themes.

"His work is so soulful," Elizabeth observed. "It's almost as if he's praying. I wish I had a clear vision of what I was meant to be and what to do with my life from now on," she mused. "I've been sitting on the fence for a long time…And I think my daughter is about to knock me off my perch."

"There's a gathering this Saturday that I'd like you to come to," Sally began. "The theme is *Unity in Diversity*. I think it would help you put things in perspective before meeting Sam's parents."

"Okay, you've got me this time, Sally. Now, how about some of those cookies?"

They went back upstairs and spent the rest of the afternoon reminiscing over their university graduating class, and the vagaries of life that had blown people in so many directions and circumstances. Sally had married Ken and they had quickly headed off to St. Lucia, where they both taught for a number of years. They had traveled in the Caribbean over a decade. Elizabeth, on the other hand, had spent some years in Newfoundland, where she had met Matt, an engineer working in the pulp and paper industry. They fell in love, moved in together and were married within six months. Michelle had been an early arrival in their marriage, but two subsequent traumatic miscarriages had severely blunted desires for a sibling for Michelle. They moved to Manitoba when Michelle was ten, and Elizabeth found to her great delight that her old college friend was also back from her escapades in the Caribbean. They had remained firm friends since. They laughed now at how a quirk of fate had Elizabeth in the Caribbean and Sally in Winnipeg.

"It's not really my place to say this, Elizabeth, but I'm going to anyway. I think Sam is a wonderful soul, with great integrity. I would be very happy if he was considering marrying one of my daughters."

"I suspect you're right, but at their young age, do you think they'll be able to overcome the differences in their family backgrounds?"

"They will. The question is, will you and will his parents?" At that, Elizabeth got up and started to give a loud, raucous rendition of *Tradition* from *Fiddler on the Roof*, twirling around the floor and finally collapsing back on the kitchen chair in a fit of laughter.

"O Lord," she said at last, "I'm in no position to stand on tradition. I have been living in a twilight zone between two cultures for the past year. I'm getting closer and closer to your notion of 'one people, one planet' all the time. I just wish there were more people who had bought into it — it would make life a lot easier."

"That's part of the excitement of it, being at the leading edge," Sally said with a conspiratorial wink.

~~~

That evening Elizabeth went with Michelle and Sam to the barn to see Jimmy, Michelle's horse. The familiar smell of horse manure mixed with harvest-fresh straw welcomed Elizabeth as she made her way down the barn to Jimmy's stall. He pricked his ears at the sound of Michelle's voice and nickered softly as she approached.

"How's my handsome boy?" she said, stroking the velvet smooth hair on his prominent blaze. "He's looking good," Elizabeth said, after her keen eye appraised his sleek coat and conditioned muscles.

Michelle groomed him with powerful strokes of the body brush. His chestnut coat glistened a burnished gold. Sam arrived with the saddle and bridle, passing them to Michelle. She quickly tacked up, finishing with protective wraps on all four legs. "Okay, let's show Mom just how much you've improved since she last saw you," Michelle said to her equine partner. She led him out of his stall and into a large fenced paddock with jumps.

Elizabeth swept her eyes over the outlying fields, heavy

with straw-gold barley bending in the evening breeze, and shimmering in the shifting light of the evening. On the western horizon, the fields had already been harvested and the shorn stubble beckoned to her equine passion. She drifted into another state, suspended between the past and the present. While her daughter carefully warmed up her horse in the foreground, stretching and warming up muscles before testing them, Elizabeth galloped away across the stubble on a sleek and swift thoroughbred. She was followed closely by Matt, who was pacing his mount and saving him for a sneaky sprint before the end of the field. But Elizabeth knew his game well and she shifted her weight slightly, opening up her horse's long stride and widening the gap between them. The result was a neck-to-neck finish, then a slow deceleration to a hand gallop, allowing exhilarated horses a chance to catch their breath. Eventually, they dropped down to a trot and then to a walk. The horses dropped their heads and stretched their necks, snorting in long, deep-throated contentment, while the riders, in deep and intimate conversation, basked in the perfection of the moment.

"Put up some warm-up fences for me, please," Michelle said, dragging her mother back to the present. Sam was ready with poles and standards, and between them, they quickly set up a warm-up grid.

"She's got you well trained," Elizabeth said. "I'm impressed."

"I love to watch them, this is the beauty of physics in motion," Sam said, as Michelle and Jimmy easily negotiated the grid with fluid motion. "I've taken pictures of the two of them at every stage of the jumping sequence, from the powerful squatting of the haunches before takeoff, to the stretch and balance of the neck arcing over a wide triple. That horse really tries for her. Brains and brawn, honed into a partnership, where the only thing they have in common is heart, bonded in single intent to make it through the course."

"Oh, there is definite hope for you," Elizabeth said. "I detect the subtle, hallowed tones and exaggerated hype of a man close to equine addiction."

Michelle rounded the corner at the end of the paddock and

made another flawless entry through the grid. "Okay, we're ready," she said bringing Jimmy to a halt in the center. "Have you picked a course for me, Mom?"

Elizabeth eyed the layout of the fences and gave her daughter an eight-fence course with two combinations, choosing easy, forgiving lines.

Michelle saluted, and set off with the focus and determination that helped her bring the young horse to his present level of training. Jimmy's ears pricked and his muscles bulged as his gait collected and steadied down the first line and through the first two fences. The next two fences required a change of direction and lead. Jimmy got the flying change with ease at the corner, and the pair negotiated the next three fences with flow and pizzazz.

Elizabeth could see that the gangly horse she had bought for Michelle two years ago had matured both physically and mentally. His form had improved tremendously. His knees now tucked carefully over the fences and his fiery spirit was more concentrated on performance and less rebellious.

The last line was through a triple combination where the ground sloped down to the first fence. This type of set-up tended to encourage a horse to lengthen his stride and get sucked in too close to the base of the first fence. Elizabeth could see the horse lengthen as he made his approach. Two strides out Michelle sat deep and tall and checked his stride, so that he shortened just before takeoff. He successfully negotiated the first part of the combination and then had to really stretch to make the second two fences.

"Well done!" said Michelle, clapping him on the neck as he cleared the last fence. "That was my fault," she confessed. "But he got me out of trouble."

"Yes," Elizabeth agreed. "Why don't you try that last combination again, but try not to lengthen on the approach this time. Keep a more even striding."

Michelle headed off again, this time making the necessary adjustment before the approach, and riding down through the combination with form and ease.

"You can't ask for better than that," Elizabeth said. "I'd finish on that if I were you."

"Yes, I'm really pleased," Michelle agreed as she swung down off the saddle and started to walk him out, loosening the girth and the nose-band. "Bet you'd like to ride him, Mom!"

"Maybe next time," Elizabeth said. "Just to feel his flat work, but he's your jumping partner. You've done a great job, Michelle."

CHAPTER 20

The next four weeks brought a slow slipping into a familiar groove, as contented, easy living wove a seductive caul around Elizabeth's raw nerves and questioning soul. But visible reminders of other worlds would periodically scratch through the thin membrane, exposing her personal angst: a neglected neighborhood driven through by accident; pan handlers on the corner of Portage and Main; construction crews working on a gas line, blue portable outhouses testifying to workplace health and safety laws. All served to prod her retreating self from its imposed silence to a weak whispering. This bond she felt with Josef — what was its origin? They could barely communicate. It wasn't just language; it was a whole context for being in the world. Physically, they had hardly touched, except for a taxi ride. A ride, where he accompanied her to the bridge that would bring her back to her world, sever her from his — the future unknown, seemingly hopeless. She banished him from her thoughts; it was a luxury she couldn't afford. The mommy genes now firmly in control, Elizabeth struggled with the possibility of her daughter's marriage and her future in-laws.

The Ketners had arrived and were staying with cousins who were hosting the bar mitzvah on Saturday, for which the cream suit had been purchased. Sharon Ketner had a brief luncheon with Elizabeth, Michelle, and Sam on the Thursday, at which time she had been charming to Elizabeth, friendly towards Michelle, and impatient with Sam.

"Is your research finished yet, Samuel? We could do with some extra help in the business. Your brothers are planning an expansion in the Toronto office."

Sam had been evasive, not wanting to upset his mother who clearly wasn't going to entertain the idea of him staying on in Manitoba after he was finished. "I'm looking at a number of possible projects across Canada," he'd said.

"We have projects that require engineers, you should talk to Ben. No need to go wandering around the place looking for work when we need you at home base."

Sam had changed the subject, but this had brought them down a more treacherous route as Sharon recounted the fortunes of a number of old family friends, some who had flourished and some who were floundering.

"Remember Beth Cohen?" she began. "She used to go to summer camp with you and Ben for years. She married that Turkish hotelier she met on holidays two years ago. It was a disaster. She came home last month completely demoralized, vowing never to return to Turkey. The man had turned into a tyrant. She should have stayed here and married that nice Joshua Steinberg. He had his eye on her since grade school."

And so it went, with those who had thrown their lot into the well-worn groove, buffeted from the vagaries of an uncertain world, while the thrill-seekers had perished or were in imminent peril. All this was revealed implicitly through well-timed pauses, intonations and the raising of eyebrows.

"I'm so pleased you're both coming to the bar mitzvah," she said at last, and with genuine warmth, turning her attention to Elizabeth and Michelle. "Would you like us to pick you up?"

"That's okay, Mother," Sam interjected, "I'm collecting them."

"You're not coming with us then?" she asked in dismay.

"No, you're going to be there way too early and I have some test sites to look in on before I go."

"Well, don't be late," she warned.

She then asked Elizabeth about St. Georges, and Michelle about her studies and future plans. Michelle told her that she was thinking of transferring over to the engineering faculty, as a number of her courses could be credited. Michelle then asked her if there was an equivalent ceremony for girls in the Jewish faith as the bar mitzvah for boys. Sharon explained that this was a celebration of taking on full religious obligations – that it was not traditionally celebrated by girls, but that many young girls now also made similar commitments. She approved of the new recognition of women in the practice of her faith.

"A break with tradition can be good sometimes then, Mother," Sam said.

"We're talking here about redecorating the cake, not turning it into a trifle, Samuel," she spoke with the deftness of one who had defended her position many times. At this she had taken her leave so that she would be on time for her next appointment. Her perfumed scent hung over the three for the remainder of the rendezvous, a reminder of her tenacity.

"That was a bit tense," Michelle admitted after she had left.

"She loved you two," Sam assured them. "It's me she's cross with. I've clearly taken a wrong turn somewhere, or am about to, and she thinks that somehow she's responsible."

"Change takes time to get used to," Elizabeth reflected.

~~~

The bar mitzvah was a spectacular mix of the sacred, the urbane, and the riotously celebratory. The religious observance was solemn, with the young man reciting from the Torah in Hebrew.

Elizabeth had difficulty following the ceremony. She found herself absentmindedly counting the number of yarmulkes in the pews ahead of her and dividing them into color groups, wondering if color had any particular significance. The man dressed in a dark suit with the black felt one that had a band threaded with gold, was he perhaps a rabbi? He was following the ceremony with an attitude of intense reverence and apparently had an aura around him, judging from the extra space allotted him by the others in his pew. There were a number of simple wine and black satin ones, whose appearance and sit seemed perfunctory at best. The Orthodox seemed to have their own personalized ones, but was there a code in the patterns like the tartans on a Scottish kilt? This was all so foreign to her. She knew so little. What did all this mean for the future of her daughter?

And then came the chant of the cantor. The human voice, articulated with musical intonation, had the power to transcend outward form and connect the hearts. Elizabeth prayed silently and felt the pull of Mosaic law and the mighty authority it had yielded through the ages. It was the same power and authority that had pervaded her own Catholic upbringing, and though she had long been estranged from the rituals of that faith, a sense of the sacred and a need to worship was stronger in her now than perhaps ever before.

The *Unity in Diversity* workshop she had attended at Sally's behest had explored patterns of religion throughout history, and the essential spiritual principles common to them all. In a workshop setting, it had been interesting but academic. Here, surrounded by people with whom she thought she had little in common, she felt a bond — perhaps ephemeral, held together by the cantor's glue — but it gave her hope and courage.

She looked at Sam, with his borrowed black satin yarmulke, and Michelle, with the suit that might never be seen again as a coordinate, paying their dues in an act of love for each other and respect for their parents. She felt blessed.

"*Shalom aleicheim*," came the final blessing and the slow procession moved down the aisle. The people nodded and smiled, removing the wall of silence like ice breaking before an Arctic ship's bows. The rest of the congregation followed in its wake in easy conversation, remarking on this or that particular highlight of the ceremony.

The banquet was laid out in a receiving hall. There was a spread of dainties and hors d'oeuvres laid out on different tables throughout the room, each table decorated with various biblical motifs.

Sam brought Elizabeth and Michelle around to meet some of his relatives — in particular, an Aunt Ruby, who wasn't really an aunt. She was a first cousin of his father's, who had a special relationship with Sam and could be counted on to react favorably to most of Sam's doings and to all of his friends. She had already heard about Michelle, and gave her a warm fleshy embrace. She had an air of assurance that comes from being old enough to say what you want and well practiced in using the privilege. This was mellowed by a personal warmth and charm that emanated from bright eyes, peering out from under a heavily-wrinkled brow.

"Michelle, I know you already, come sit by me and tell me how Sam has been behaving. He hasn't come to see me in ages," she said, throwing a disparaging look at Sam, who smiled broadly and then kissed her on the forehead. He then excused himself while he went to get some drinks for everybody.

Aunt Ruby had commandeered an advantageous position from which to watch the crowd and invited Elizabeth and Michelle to join her. She then proceeded to give them a run down of the Ketner family tree, and who was who and what was what at the bar mitzvah. Aunt Ruby was the perfect companion for the uninitiated. She attracted people like a magnet and used the opportunity to introduce both Michelle and Elizabeth to as many people as possible.

"Bourke? You're not related to Matt Bourke by any chance?" A bearded and strikingly handsome man in his late forties, asked.

"Yes," a startled Elizabeth replied. "He's my husband – my late husband." She had no recollection of ever having met this man before.

"Late husband? Matt has died? I had no idea. I'm terribly sorry," he stumbled in embarrassment.

"That's okay," Elizabeth assured him. "It's over two years ago now."

"I'm David Cristall. I worked with your husband on the Pine Falls project about four years ago. We pulled a number of late-nighters together. I really liked him. I moved to Toronto shortly afterwards and lost touch with him."

Elizabeth racked her brain to try and dig out the name David Cristall from the recesses, but to no avail. She smiled at him, and that gave him the encouragement to continue.

"Well, he may not have mentioned me to you, but he certainly talked about you to me. Lots."

"Now I'm really at a disadvantage," Elizabeth said. "You had better tell me something about yourself, Mr. Cristall, to even things up a bit."

"I'm a corporate lawyer, worked for years with Merchants and Ross, but went freelance just before the Pine Falls project," he began. "Henry is an associate of mine and was kind enough to invite me to this celebration," he concluded as a way of explaining his presence.

"Funny how men always define themselves primarily by their work," Elizabeth stated unguardedly.

He blushed and looked a little flustered.

"I'm sorry, I didn't intend to be rude," she apologized. "It's just that Matt's being an engineer seems the least important memory I hold of him. But the fact that he loved children, had a keen sense of humor, and was a complete clod around the house are ever-present memories."

"Let me start again," he said, and he looked at her with fresh curiosity. "May I present myself. I'm David Cristall, recently divorced, father of two wonderful boys ages twelve and fourteen. I love squash and sailing, hate traffic jams, and am trying desperately to develop a sense of humor to survive the teen years. Now we're more than even." He gave her a dry smile.

Now Elizabeth was somewhat embarrassed and wondered which part of his disclosure she should pick up on. "Well, I rarely get upset in traffic these days," she said opting for the safest entry. "Unless there's a funeral, there is never more than three cars in a row to be seen in St. Georges."

"St. Georges? That's in the Caribbean, isn't it? What brought you there?"

"I'm a teacher at one of the schools there."

"Ah, yes, but you can teach here. What brought you there?"

Elizabeth realized that things were about to go deeper than party chit-chat when Sam reappeared and asked Elizabeth to please come and meet his father.

Elizabeth started to say goodbye to David Cristall, who protested that she owed him at least one personal disclosure before she left him. "I'm naturally reserved," she said, "but am becoming more audacious, unguarded, and a little insensitive with the passing of time. Please forgive me."

She left him standing with a bemused look on his face.

Isaac Ketner was a short, balding man, impeccably groomed in a charcoal gray suit and patent shoes. His remarkably blue eyes lit up as Sam ushered Elizabeth to him. He clasped her hands warmly in his, welcoming her to the celebration, and thanking her for her attendance.

"Henry is my cousin's youngest child and only son. He has been looking forward to this bar mitzvah for a long time. It was a good excuse to come and visit Sam also. We miss him," he said. "But his interests are different and he has worked hard. I'm proud of him," he added with affection. "And you have a very talented daughter, Mrs. Bourke. You must be proud of her also?"

"Yes, I am," she replied. "She and Sam have become very close. How do you feel about that, Mr. Ketner?" she asked, confirming her own suspicions of her recently acquired impudence.

"Such a nice girl, but they are so young, don't you think?" he hedged.

"Yes, they are young," she agreed. "And also determined."

"You've met my wife, Mrs. Bourke. Now, there's determined! Samuel comes by it honestly."

"What has she determined? Your wife, I mean."

He looked at her with inquisitive eyes, tempered with wisdom and compassion. "My dear Mrs. Bourke, that answer has a long history. You and I will have lunch together next week and then we will have a long talk. Today, we enjoy the festivities. Have a good look at us, see what you think." And he took her by the arm to introduce her to Henry's father.

CHAPTER 21

Elizabeth leaned up against the fence to get a better view of the jumps.

"Number forty-eight is now entering the ring. Jimminy Cricket. Owned and ridden by Michelle Bourke," came the announcement over the loud speaker.

Jimmy trotted in, tail high and neck arched. His ears flicked from side to side as he interpreted his surroundings. He baulked slightly as he passed by a wide oxer, built out of staring white panels with red diamond insets. Elizabeth noticed Michelle check him sharply with an outside rein. "Relax, Michelle," she whispered under her breath, as she mentally started to ride the course with her daughter. Michelle took a wide sweeping circle to collect and focus Jimmy before making her approach to the first line. Good girl, Elizabeth thought, and she held her breath while thirteen hundred pounds of snorting equine energy attacked the first three fences, over-jumping all three with nervous enthusiasm.

"Oh boy, he's wound up," she exclaimed softly in a nervous giggle.

"They're looking pretty good," came a voice from over her left shoulder. She swung around and to her amazement saw David Cristall, who she thought looked pretty good himself, in a pair of designer jeans, beautifully tooled cowboy boots, and an open-necked white shirt.

"My son has just finished competing in the pony ring. I heard Michelle's name being called over the loud speaker, so I wandered over to see how she was doing."

"Hi!" she said, and then refocused her attention on the ring.

Jimmy had successfully negotiated every fence so far, but the partnership was a bit tenuous as he fought for control, raising his head to evade Michelle's hand. They rounded the corner for the last two fences, Michelle pushing Jimmy hard into the corner to gain some time to balance him and regain his attention. It worked. His head lowered in submission and his powerful hindquarters collected under him. They approached the red and white oxer with focus. Three strides out, he started to wiggle as his courage waned before the evil-looking fence. Michelle focused beyond the fence to safety, and Jimmy followed, taking off long and sailing over the oxer with feet to spare. There was a gasp from the crowd and then applause as they cleared the last fence.

"Yes!" Elizabeth shouted and she let out a whoop of joy and relief.

David Cristall's eyes sparkled as they met hers and he laughed at her exuberance, revealing a set of well cared-for white teeth, adorned with two gold crowns.

"Not pretty, but it worked," Elizabeth laughed, and she headed for the out gate to congratulate Michelle. Sam beat her to it; by the time Elizabeth got there, Michelle had already dismounted, run her stirrups up, and was walking Jimmy out with one hand, her other arm wrapped around Sam.

"That was a bit of a scary round, Mom," she beamed at Elizabeth. "What will I do for the jump-off?"

"Forget about the time, just go for a nice, slow, controlled clear."

"Well done, Michelle."

"Thanks, Mr. Cristall. How's Joel making out?" Michelle asked David, who had followed Elizabeth to the out gate.

"He's doing okay. He's got a good pony."

"You didn't tell me you were interested in horses," Elizabeth quipped, stopping to allow him catch up.

"I'm not," he confessed. "That's my ex-wife's passion. But Joel likes it and I promised I'd come and watch."

"That's a pretty good reason."

"Yes, and I had better get back or I'll miss his next class." He moved closer and lowered his voice. "Will you have dinner with me tonight?" he asked.

She looked blankly, stunned by the completely unexpected invitation.

"Why not?" she said at last. It was as much a question for herself as an affirmative for him.

"Pick you up at eight?"

"Do you know where I live?" she laughed.

"I have my sources."

"Okay, see you at eight."

~~~

Michelle's next round had gone according to plan, with a more relaxed Jimmy completing the course in a fluid but slow time. This had put them in third place, which had more than satisfied Michelle.

"I'm really happy, Mom. Life is just about perfect for me right now," she had announced on their way home. "Sam's father is a sweetheart and I think I can get along with his mother," she continued. "I'm going to spend a week with them before school reopens, at their family cabin on Lake of the Woods. So I guess we'll really find out then."

Elizabeth reflected on the evening she had spent with Sam's father, and how the compassionate and pragmatic little man had impressed her. During the first course, he had inquired about her life on the islands, and how she coped without a family network. He then went on to talk about his family and how central it was to them — especially to Sharon. She had lost all her immediate family in the holocaust, and had arrived in Toronto a frightened and bewildered little girl of seven. She had been brought up by a maiden aunt who showered her with love and cocooned her from any further injury by an indifferent post-war Canada. She cherished her family and had the fierceness of a lioness when it came to protecting her children and defending their right to proclaim their Jewishness. They weren't strictly Orthodox and demonstrated a definite laxity in the observance of many of the laws. But they treasured their social and spiritual heritage. Anybody who would become a member of their family would need to be able to understand and appreciate the significance of this.

"And that, my dear Elizabeth, may not be all that easy — especially for one who, up until now, has had no exposure to us and all our little quirks."

"Well, I'm impressed with Sam, and with you too, Isaac," Elizabeth had replied warmly.

"Sam is an easy sell. But me and my dear Sharon, now that takes more maturity."

They both laughed and fell into chit-chat over dessert. Finally, during coffee, he'd said, "Some things take time and some things just need a little coaxing. I think your Michelle and my Sharon need to spend a little time together. And I know just the right place."

~ ~ ~

The man was definitely intellectually stimulating. Conversation came easy with him, and he vividly described some of the more exotic places he had visited. He had been to Mombai and Timbuktu, he had stood on the Great Wall of China, and read the *New York Times* while floating on his back on the Dead Sea, places that Matt and Elizabeth had only dreamed of visiting. He was so gracious and attentive as she rattled on about life in St. Georges, that she at once felt both warm and unnerved. By the time the dessert trolley rolled around, she was flushed by both the wine and the heady talk. He spoke about a business trip that would take him to the Caribbean in November, and how he would like to visit St. Georges on the way back. That is, if she would promise to show him around.

"All twelve square miles of it?" she laughed.
"All twelve square miles of it."
"I think I could fit that in during my lunch hour."

He said he'd heard the sailing was really good down there and he might try and charter a yacht. The evening was an elixir, with the right amount of delectable food and charming company. It induced a carefree suspension of grief for past losses or present worries.

Over coffee, he told her of a trip to Haiti, and the wonders of Creole cooking and the exotic pleasures of the Petionville area of Port au Prince. The picture he painted was real enough: haute cuisine, exotic nightclubs, complete with some tourist voodoo. But it was very different from her experience there. She then told him of Gustaf and Marie, thinking she might in some way reveal a crack in the smooth exterior. But, though he registered some shock and sympathy at their predicament, the tale seemed to increase his interest in her, and he became more intimate in his overtures.

"You're not my type, you know," he said quietly. "But I

find you most intriguing."

It had been so long since Elizabeth was paid this kind of attention by a man that she couldn't discern whether it was genuine or flattery. But the ambience was perfect; she enjoyed both the evening and his company. She told him as much.

As he dropped her off at the apartment, she gave him a warm yet noncommittal embrace and kiss on the cheek.

"I'm leaving next week on a two-week business trip so I won't get a chance to see you again before you return to St. Georges. But I will pay a visit to St. Georges in November if you give me even the slightest bit of encouragement. What do you say, Elizabeth?"

"I'd be happy to see you. St. Georges may not be the most exotic place you've traveled to. Still, it does have its own charm. It's worth a visit."

"Expect me in November then," he said, and he bent forward and kissed her on the forehead.

~~~

Elizabeth looked at her watch. It was eleven o'clock. She sneaked upstairs to the second-floor apartment, hoping her daughter had already gone to bed. It was the first time that anyone had asked her out since Matt's death. It was clear that David Cristall found her not only good company, but attractive. She wondered what exactly it was he saw in her. He was unquestionably handsome: the facial symmetry of a Greek god, dark nut-brown eyes set in golden skin, and rich black, wavy hair that had only started to gray around the temples.

She carefully placed the key in the lock, turning it slowly.

"Is that you, Mom?" came a sleepy voice.

Shit! Elizabeth thought, and she felt like a schoolgirl being caught breaking her curfew. "Yes, it's me," she whispered, and she rammed the key home with a noisy jangling of metal on metal.

Elizabeth went to the kitchen and put the kettle on. She would have a cup of tea and give Michelle a chance to get back to sleep before joining her. She went to the bathroom and examined herself in the mirror. She had a haircut before the bar mitzvah, and the streaks of gray were now colored in red highlights (upon the insistence of a very persuasive stylist). Sharon Ketner had recommended him after Elizabeth had commented favorably on her hair. She had been horrified at the cost of the hairdo, and it had completely dampened her enthusiasm for the end result. But now, looking in the mirror, she could see the lift it had given her. Her eyes were bright, and the bags that had been sagging under them on her return had melted away. Six weeks in Canada had definitely shored her up.

She slowly sipped her tea and looked through the pages of the large family album that had been entrusted to Michelle. Images of summers by the lake and winters skiing. Horses in fuzzy winter coats and horses in sleek summer coats. Friends at this or that gathering. Everything with a backdrop of material security and ease. Then she looked at photographs of St. Georges. Rusting tin-roofed shacks, side-by-side with brightly colored ones. Donkeys shading themselves under the casuarina trees. The open smiles and beaming eyes of the school children. Images that all warmed her heart.

She knew she was ready to go back. Psychologically and intellectually, she was inextricably linked with the material reality depicted in the large album. Still, it was slowly becoming clear to her that her heart and soul had been captivated by the spirit and the urgency of the daily effort of "trying to make it" partially revealed on the Kodak paper of her most recent snaps.

How these two realities would accommodate each other was far less clear.

Part III

HAITI

CHAPTER 22

"Je m'excuse," the woman apologized as she slid her crate of sodas up to the front of the tap-tap, ramming the side of it into Elizabeth's foot. Her thick leather hiking boots had helped take the sting out of the encounter, but the point of her ankle had taken some punishment. She quickly jerked her foot out of the way, stowing it behind a sack of flour. She nodded and smiled at the woman, and inched her way further down the seat to try and make more room.

The man to her right was sitting with his feet hanging over the side so that he could jump on and off quickly. He had a fist full of filthy bank notes in one hand and a rounded stone in the other. He was the conductor; the one who collected the money and whose job it was to alert the driver to either stop or go. His eyes were yellow and sunken in the hollows of his emaciated face, his skin stretched tightly over his skull. His shoulder bumped against Elizabeth as the tap-tap swerved to avoid the huge craters and oncoming traffic. It pressed through his fleshless skin and knocked against her padded shoulders with the resonance of a thick stick. He avoided looking at her, but she felt his awareness of her. She remembered Claire and wondered how many offspring he was driven to support while time allowed.

About two miles from Milot, a young man on the opposite side of the tap-tap spoke to her in English, asking if she was going to La Citadelle and if she needed a guide.

"Non, merci," she replied in French.

"Pas touriste?" he asked with surprise.

"Pas touriste," she confirmed, and silently prayed that Sister Thérèse would be waiting for her at the turnaround in Milot as promised. He was the third person who had tried to attach himself to her as a guide since she arrived in Cap Hatien earlier that day.

~~~

She had decided to go to Milot alone this time to see how she would cope on her own. She found the tap-tap stand without too much difficulty. But she waited for an hour before the right one came along, sheltering under a street vendor's soiled canvas during a downpour, which splashed up large gobs of filth from the mud-encrusted street.

The street vendor, a large woman with powerful looking arms and a massive bottom, was tending to an assortment of bubbling pots and charcoal grills. She beckoned Elizabeth over, showing her an oily-looking stew of unrecognizable vittles. Before she had time to decline, the heavens opened, unleashing the short but drenching downpour. Elizabeth quickly accepted the vendor's invitation of shelter, scuttling under the canvas with half a dozen others. It was in the cramped space of the shelter that she had been first approached by a young man with an offer of assistance. She artfully declined, using her complete collection of Creole phrases in rapid succession, creating the illusion of fluency and familiarity with the country.

It had worked. The street vendor had a great laugh at the young man's expense, slapping him on the back with one hand, while ladling Elizabeth out a helping of her evil-looking stew with the other. The concoction presented itself to her as a test of her authenticity, and Elizabeth accepted. Under the direct scrutiny of the vendor, she scooped up the first spoonful with apparent relish. To her surprise, it tasted a good deal better than it looked, and she'd managed to make a getaway without blowing her cover.

~~~

It was the last run of the day, and the afternoon sun was tempered by large gray clouds that had rolled down from the mountain slopes. Elizabeth could smell the red earth in the moist air, and the scent of fruiting trees wafted intermittently into the crowded air space of the tap-tap. She could smell the bodies around her, some sweet and laced with fragrance, the scent of visitors returning home. Others were sour with the pungent sweat of a day's work.

But the dying man beside her had no smell, as if he had shed his animal core and was already spirit waiting to break free of his rusting cage to fly into the heavens. When the tap-tap took a particularly ugly lurch to the right, Elizabeth instinctively shot her arm out to provide some support. He grabbed the side of the driver's cab and alarm filled his vacant eyes. Their combined action stabilized him, and he banged his rounded stone down hard on the side of the tap-tap and raged at the driver to slow down.

"Careful, mwen ami," Elizabeth soothed. She released her hold and he looked at her with wild eyes. Before her soft gaze, they transformed into calm liquid pools, quiet desperation reflected from their depths.

"Mèsi," he said at last, and he held her gaze for one long searing instant as their souls made a momentary encounter, destined to stay etched in both their memories.

The tap-tap came to the turnaround point and emptied itself of its assortment of humanity. The would-be guide got out ahead of Elizabeth and waited to one side, assisting her with her backpack as she climbed down. No one was there to meet her, but she could see the school in the distance and decided to start walking.

"Where are you going? I can help," he suggested.

"I am visiting friends," she replied evasively while she gathered her thoughts. How could she shake him off without coming across as an arrogant, obnoxious *blanche*?

Her problem was solved by the friendly honking of a white, rust-streaked mini van, driven by Sister Thérèse and partially filled with six beaming children. It stopped with a jolt and the side door slid open. Gustaf and Marie burst forth and ran towards her. She opened her arms wide and gathered them both into a giggling, ecstatic embrace.

The guide looked at them and then at Sister Thérèse. "Pas touriste," he informed her, and then turned and disappeared down a side street.

"Bienvenue, Elizabeth," the soft-spoken missionary said.

"Merci," Elizabeth replied as she climbed into the mini-van. Gustaf cleared the other children to make sure that he and

Marie would be seated next to her. He sat upright, with an attitude of proud possession, while Marie brushed close to her, leaning her trusting little body against her arms. Elizabeth put her arm around Marie and let her nestle against her, on the pretext of making more room. But they both knew it was because she really cared.

The little van jolted along the cobbled streets, and the children sang a song, in which the verse changed each time a child was dropped off. By the time they got back to the school, Marie was asleep and Gustaf was telling Elizabeth how good his reading was, and how he got first place in the math test they had last week.

"But the spelling is still not too good," Sister Thérèse commented.

"That's because Gustaf thinks so fast," Elizabeth explained, remembering his enthusiastic but inaccurate approach to work.

She carried Marie inside rather than wake her up. "Gosh, she's very light," Elizabeth said.

"She's been sick. We're going to get a blood test done," Sister Thérèse said quietly.

A chill ran down Elizabeth's spine, and she examined the sleeping child for tell-tale signs of ill health. But she looked fine. A bit frail perhaps, but she always looked that way. Elizabeth compared this porcelain doll with her full brother: he seemed to have aged six months in two, pubescent hormones stretching his body and filling out his muscles, while she had remained a child.

"Their aunt has gone to Gonaives to look after her father who is ill," Sister Thérèse explained. "Henri has work there also at the moment. We agreed to have the children stay with us while she was away. We have extra room here at the moment."

Sister Thérèse handed Elizabeth a plain brown envelope without any stamp. "This letter arrived here for you about two weeks ago." There was a Port au Prince address in one corner, with a message for the bearer to please deliver it to the sisters at Milot. Elizabeth's name was clearly marked across the front. The tidy, copper-plate writing was unmistakably Josef's.

"Can I stay with you for a few days, while I visit with the

children?" she asked. "Of course, I will pay for my board."

"How about taking Sr. Paulette's class for a few days. That would more than compensate for your board. She is away for four days. Her young assistant can help with translation."

"I'll give it a shot," Elizabeth agreed.

~~~

The mission house was a squat concrete building in the same yard as the school. The kitchen opened out into a spacious, dining-living area with two concrete walls. The two open sides were screened to keep out the mosquitoes. Six little bedrooms opened off a long narrow corridor. Only four were presently filled, as the sisters' forces had dwindled. Gustaf and Marie were occupying the other two temporarily, but the hope was for some new postulants to fill the vacancies. They would put an extra cot in Marie's room for Elizabeth while she was with them.

Marie started to shift from her curled up position on the couch, and she soon sat up, blinking tired eyes in a confused return to consciousness. "Tante Elizabeth?" she said at last, searching around the room for the object of her desire.

"Ici, ma petite," Elizabeth hailed from the kitchen where she had gone to see if she could help.

Marie quickly got up off the couch and skipped into the kitchen. Elizabeth passed her some knives and forks and they both started to set the table.

"Have you forgotten all your English, Marie?" Elizabeth asked.

"No!" Gustaf interjected. It was his job to feed the goat, and he entered into the conversation as he passed through to the porch with a small plate of yam and plantain peelings. "We read our books and practice every night."

"Good, you can read me a story tonight then, Gustaf."

Supper was a modest but healthy meal of chicken soup, served with a side dish of fried sweet plantain and mashed yams. A bowl of oranges was passed around for dessert. The conversation centered around the school, and Elizabeth talked with the young nun who would be helping her with the class tomorrow. She was a local girl who the nuns had educated. She had joined the little community straight out of school.

Elizabeth would take the grade one class. Not a group she felt very skilled at handling, but at least the language difficulty would be less of a barrier to teaching. She could probably handle alphabet introduction and simple math in Creole, with a little bit of help.

After supper, the nuns went to their little chapel for evening prayer. Elizabeth took the opportunity to spend some time alone with the children. They had had a good summer and had spent most of it running free with the other children who lived on the mountainside. The Citadelle had lots of tourists that summer and the children had earned a little bit of money bringing fruit and drinks to them as they made their way up the mountainside. They were very impressed that the children could speak English. Cheeko, one of the horse guides, had let Gustaf accompany him once or twice so that he could chat to the tourists en route. Some of the tourists had tipped him. He was saving his money to buy a hat like the one Cheeko wore, felt not woven.

Marie, who had been quiet but attentive to her brother's chatter, passed Elizabeth a large black note book. It contained her schoolwork, which was commendable. On one page, marked with a star, was a short story. It was written in English.

What I want to be

When I get big, I want to be a teacher.
I will teach the boys and girls to read and rite.
Reading is a lot of fun and it helps you learn things.
My favorit teacher is Mrs. Bourke. She is very nice.
That's why I want to be a teacher.

Write   Favorite
Write   Favorite
Write   Favorite

Elizabeth winked at her and told her that she was very proud of her, and that she was going to be a very good teacher.

"I'm going to own my own horses and bring the tourists up to La Citadelle and make lots of dollars," Gustaf announced.

~ ~ ~

Chère Elizabeth, how are you? I had no possibility to send you a letter until now.
Your address was lost. I had much difficulties. My Mother, she died. I was very sad.
Now my news is good. I have a work permit and go back to St. Georges. I miss you.

God keep you safe
Josef

Elizabeth re-read the simple letter for the third time. What difficulties did he have? In Haiti, that could be a multitude. How did he get the work permit? The simple phrase, "I miss you," caused a flood of warm memories: his delight in the simplest of pleasures, his thoughtfulness, his transcendent faith. She longed for his radiant smile and the lilt of his voice.

CHAPTER 23

Josef's summer had been one of grinding toil, complicated by the slow healing of his torn shoulder muscles. He had taken no time off work, as that would have meant rapid replacement. He wore a sling whenever he could, but otherwise forced the reluctant and painful tissue into action. This resulted in recurrent bouts of inflammation, which burst into flames in the dog hours of the night when he yearned for sleep. But eventually the bouts became less frequent and the pain less intense, and he thanked God for his good fortune to have work and to be earning some money.

When the work was finished on that site, the foreman had told Josef to turn up at another site in two weeks when work was due to start. He took the opportunity to go back to Gonaives to visit his family.

The mango and plantain trees were still offering both shade and fruit, and his family celebrated his return by picking and preparing a variety of dishes from the fruitful branches.

One of the swaggering young roosters, which had terrorized their yard, had been stealthily dispatched and roasted. This particular fowl had attacked Josef's brother, on more than one occasion, by launching himself from the corrugated tin roof of the outhouse and burying his rapidly developing spurs into the back of Jean's neck. This turned a visit to the outhouse into a perilous escapade. The rooster had successfully occupied the outhouse for the previous month, and defended it against all intruders who approached without suitable defense. The children had given up using the outhouse altogether, and the only thing that had spared the wretched creature's life thus far was his youth and extreme deftness in disappearing rapidly into the undergrowth whenever Jean had a machete in his hand.

Finally, Jean had commissioned one of the neighbor's children, who was artful with a slingshot, to dispatch the tyrant, promising him two of the large mangos that drooped ripe and luscious from the tree. The boy had patiently skulked in the undergrowth behind the shed, and had delivered an unmerciful coup de grace with his slingshot, while the over-confident fowl was preening himself on the shed roof. The blow had been serious but not fatal, and the wounded rooster had staggered towards the bush seconds after he had been hit. The boy had leapt out of the bush swinging a machete, completing his mission with one accurate swish of the blade.

Josef had arrived into the yard, unannounced and unexpected during the ensuing hooping and hollering, and his brother had quickly reconstructed the episode into a visionary preparation for his return. There had been much laughing and recounting of the affair over the feast that followed, the antics and ferocity of the deceased rooster becoming more prodigious with each account.

Kok la touye de chats, li manje yo pou dine. "That rooster killed two kittens and ate them for dinner."

Se vre? "That's true?"

Wi, se vre. "Yes, it's true."

Men-m chin an te pè li. "Even the dogs were afraid of him."

Mwen kwè li te mechan. " I think he had an evil spirit," commented Jean's twelve-year-old son.

Bien petete li ap retounen vini pran ou tou Fifi. Ou tap voye roch bali. "He might come back and take you, Fifi. You threw rocks at him."

"Sh sh," interjected Maman, who had joined the party, but was not feeling well enough to eat. She had not ventured out much in the past month, sitting instead on the step of her shanty for a few hours each morning, so that she could talk to the children and generally boss her daughter-in-law around. Since her husband died a long time past, she was the sole authority in the yard. They all knew she was ill, but she stubbornly refused any assistance. When her daughter-in-law, who still secretly believed in and practiced voodoo, had made a herbal brew for her and tacked a straw image to her door, she had flung both the brew and the charm out the door, accusing her of *obeah*. Then she banned her from coming into her shanty.

Her authority still held sway over the family group, and her grandson stopped his prattle but made a grotesque face at his sister, Fifi, in imitation of an evil spirit. Fifi shrieked.

Vini, cheri, "Come here, dear," Josef soothed and she went and sat on his knee.

Di mwen ki sa ou konnen de St. Georges, tonton. "Tell me about St. Georges, Uncle," she asked.

Josef smiled and told her a story about the beautiful blue-green sea, and the fish and conch that were so plentiful that a hook without bait could catch you a fish big enough to feed the whole family.

Ki le wap retounen, tonton? "When are you going back, uncle?" *Mwen pa konnen, cheri. Sel Bon Dye.* "I don't know, dear. Only God knows."

Later that night in his bed, Josef could hear his mother groan and twist and turn in the next room. The partition wall stopped at the eaves, and as there was no ceiling – only bare rafters – it was possible to have a conversation between the two rooms.

Maman, eske ou bien? "Mother, are you all right?"

Wi, ale kouche. "Yes, go to sleep."

The groaning stopped, but he could still hear her shifting uncomfortably in the bed.

His dreams were visited by images of Theoline, smiling and pregnant. He placed his hand on her swollen belly and waited for the little thump that reverberated with the tiny life inside. He held her close to him, brushing his cheek against hers and stroking her hair. At first she responded with soft warm skin against his, but it slowly turned hot and wet with sweat. She started to moan and her belly was no longer full. He awoke to the groans of his mother, who could no longer stifle her anguish and pain.

"Theoline!" he called out in confusion, and then "Maman!" as he leapt out of bed, fully conscious.

The old woman was burning up and she held her stomach to try to relieve the pain. He held her hand and she placed it on her stomach to show him where it hurt. He could feel a hard mass beneath the skin, and she recoiled as he tentatively tried to circumscribe it.

Mwen Dye, Maman, konbyen tan ou gen depi ou malad? "My God, Mother, how long have you had this illness?" *Nou dive ale awek ou lopital.* "We must get you to a hospital."

Pou ki sa? "For what?" she said. *Mwen fini. Rete la pou ka priye ak mwen.* "I am finished. Stay and pray with me."

And he did. He prayed the same healing prayer Elizabeth had given him when Claire was dying.

> *Ton nom est ma guerison, o mon Dieu,*
> *Et ton souvenir est mon remede.*
> *Être pres de toi est mon espoir,*
> *Et mon amour pour toi est mon compagnon.*
> *Ta misericorde est ma guerison et mon soutien en ce monde et dans l'autre. Tu es veritablement le Dieu de toute bonte, l'Omniscient, l'infiniment Sage.*
> - Bahá'u'lláh

"Thy name is my healing, O my God,
And remembrance of Thee is my remedy.
Nearness to Thee is my hope,
And love for Thee is my companion.
Thy mercy to me is my healing and my succor in both this world and the world to come.
Thou verily art the All-Bountiful, the All-Knowing, the All-Wise."
- Bahá'u'lláh

He then started to sing softly to her, a song in Creole:
> *Kretien jenn, Jesus ap rele.*
> *Ou rega la gloire ou rega sou la tere.*
> *Nou pa konnen ki jou ki le nan reveille.*
> *Krisla li fe minuit mwen ka.*
>
> *Pou ale Miami ou bezwen yon paspor.*
> *Canada St. Domingue ou bezwen yon paspor.*
> *Min pou ale na siel ou pa bezwen paspor.*
> *Seyon sel bagay se asepte Jesus.*

"Young Christians, Jesus is calling.
You look on high you look on the earth.
We know not the day or the time.
Only Christ knows the minute.

To go to Miami you need a passport.

Canada and St. Dominique you need a passport. But to go to heaven you don't need a passport. The only thing you need is to accept Jesus."

The pinched muscles around the old woman's cheeks and eyes slowly relaxed, and she eased back into sleep.

Josef kept vigil with her and drifted in his own semi-conscious state. He wondered why the women in his life first filled him with so much joy and love, then left him with pain and sorrow. He wondered why there were such great divisions between people and races, when he now knew that their hearts were the same. And he wondered why he, a simple man who knew little, thought about these things so much. He laughed to himself silently, and turned himself over with radiant acquiescence to the will of God. He went back to his bed and slept a long, deep and peaceful sleep.

When he awoke next morning, his mother was dead.

CHAPTER 24

Lennox was furious with Robinson. "Stooped bastard," he muttered. "Always gettin' hiself into trouble." He continued mumbling to himself as he drove up to the large, two-storey house that Robinson had built and moved into two years ago. He pounded on the door, knowing full well that Robinson was probably asleep inside.

Robinson arrived at the door in sweat pants and an old T-shirt, bleary-eyed and ill-tempered. "What you want!" he barked.

"You got no damn wookers, boss, dat what," Lennox stormed. "Immigration take de best ones. Now what you goin' to do?"

Robinson's eyes cleared and narrowed as he grappled with the situation.

"I tell you fix dose permits, long time 'go," Lennox continued, releasing months of frustration with his boss.

Robinson turned on his heels and went to the bedroom to grab his keys and baseball cap. "That cousin of mine, no use," he muttered, brushing past Lennox and slamming the door behind him. "Who do we need to keep?" he demanded as he headed towards his car.

"Pierre, Claude and Josef for sure. Dey best wookers you got boss. Pierre not done dem window frames. Josef and Claude only two who do fancy plaster wok."

~~~

Robinson spent the next four hours haranguing all his political connections, especially his cousin, Harvey, who he felt owed him some favours. But this was his third offence and even Harvey had had enough of him. The only satisfaction Robinson got was the voluntary repatriation of the three mentioned, so that they could return later when and if their work permits were processed. Josef Jean Claude was the most likely to get back, because someone had already applied for a permit for him and the paperwork was at least started.

The irony was that as a native islander with a construction

business, Robinson would have had little difficulty getting permits for his workers – if he had started the process in a timely manner. Now he would have to play by the full set of rules; it would take him much longer and his business would suffer.

Lennox was aware of an underground network, which the Haitians used to convey messages back and forth between Haiti and the Islands. Still, he wasn't quite sure how it worked. Jacques hadn't elaborated but assured him that it was "no problem." He could give him the work permits when they came through and he would get them to Haiti.

By the end of the summer, Robinson was so behind in his contracts that he had dispatched Jacques back to Haiti with the three work permits and tickets for the men to fly back immediately. Jacques had successfully wrangled a permit for himself out of the deal, and had headed off to Haiti with the treasures concealed in an inside pocket of his shirt. They were like pure gold and would be paid for in full when the men returned and started working. It was a price they would be happy to pay for the security it provided.

Josef had received his work permit the day after his mother had been buried. He was in the yard helping clean up following the departure of visiting relatives, when Jacques arrived. He looked the picture of the returning exile: with a recently shaved head, new jeans and sneakers, and if his shirt wasn't exactly new, it could pass for it. He went into the yard and waited to one side while Josef gathered up some leaves he had just raked. His journey had not been without incident. He had first caught up with Claude, who lived in Cap Hatien. That had been easy. But Pierre came from a mountain village between Cap and Gonaives. It was unlikely that he would be there, as there was rarely work in the country. But his people would know of his whereabouts, so Jacques had made the journey by tap-tap and on foot.

After a four-hour journey on foot he came to a small wattle hut nestling in an aging orange grove. A barefoot, pregnant woman came to the door. When he asked about Pierre she became hysterical. With wild gesticulations she pointed to her swollen jaw and bruised arms. She claimed she had been beaten and abandoned by Pierre. Jacques looked at her swollen belly, a condition for which Pierre had no chance of being responsible. She sobbed as she told him that she had been lonely, that a woman needed a man to survive in these parts. Jacques, tired and hungry, spent the night in her home. In the early hours of the morning he was awakened by a growling menacing voice. A wild-eyed man approached him wielding a machete. He bolted through the door, barely avoiding the menacing blade of the man's machete. He galloped down the mountainside without stopping, until he came to the village on the lower slopes where he prayed the people were less crazy. He had given up on his search for Pierre and returned to Gonaives to look for Josef.

Josef spotted him in his peripheral vision, first glimpsing the new black sneakers, one lace long and dangling like a slovenly teenager, while the other was coiled and looped to attention. He slowly moved his eyes up the clean dark denim. There was something familiar in the spread of the legs and the bend of the knee that prompted Josef to speed up his scan until he made eye contact with the visitor. Jacques looked at him with wide-eyed admiration and love. He ran to embrace the man that had become a surrogate father to him during his difficult stay in St. Georges.

"I am very happy to see you," Josef said, acknowledging their common bond of English-speaking St. Georges.

"I got one work permit for you." Jacques smiled with great pride as he presented Josef's permit. Then they both collapsed into rapid and joyful Creole. Jacques told of how Mr. Robinson had gotten into big trouble with immigration this time and might even have to pay a fine, how there was a new site that needed skilled masons, and how he wanted Josef, Pierre, and Claude to return immediately.

Josef could hardly believe his ears. "Thank you, Jesus!" he proclaimed, throwing his arms up in a gesture of adoration. When Jacques told him about his problems locating Pierre, he laughed and put his arm around his shoulder assuring him that they would go together to Port au Prince and track him down.

That night Josef had prayed joyously and sung loudly as he packed his belongings. The cloud of uncertainty that had shrouded him all summer dissipated. He would be flying back to St. Georges. He would get a little house with Jacques, and they could sleep through the night without worrying about a late night knock from immigration. He would see Elizabeth again soon. That would be nice. Yes, that would be very nice. And he sat down and took out his French/English dictionary, and methodically worked his way through the language maze until he was satisfied with the few short lines he had written in English.

~~~

Goodbyes are often joyous occasions in Haiti, signifying a passage of hope for both those leaving and those left behind. There were no tears when the two men left, but lots of excitement and banter as a small group of neighbors came over to wish them well. They admired the work permits and sent greetings to their own relatives working in St. Georges.

Josef and Jacques left the yard with letters from wives and girlfriends, all hoping to join their men as soon as the men could send for them. The assembled group teased the two men, wondering if they had girlfriends in St. Georges or in Haiti, or maybe in both places. Josef laughed and Jacques' black skin shaded to purple as one of the young women flirted with him shamelessly. They boarded the bus to Port au Prince. It rattled its way down the city streets and out into the countryside, where it made its winding, tortuous trip to the nation's capital.

Port au Prince – noisy, dirty, and choked with traffic and people – greeted them with the usual chaos. A broken-down bus had turned a busy street into a bottleneck, causing the two lanes to converge into one. A driver in an oncoming bus had stopped to see if he could help. The two drivers leaned out of their respective vehicles, which were within scraping distance of each other, and conversed for what seemed like an interminable length, while the rising tide of traffic behind them honked and spewed out poisonous fumes from idling vehicles. The exchange was completed when the two men slapped each other on the shoulders and six passengers from the crippled vehicle squeezed their way into the functioning bus. It then heaved its way past the bottleneck and continued on its way, the driver unruffled by the indignation hurled at him from the drivers piled up behind it.

~~~

Josef made a list of the construction sites he knew of in Port au Prince, and he and Jacques decided to split up in their search for Pierre. They would rendezvous later that evening in the park across from the Presidential Palace.

Josef had found Pierre on his third stop. He was sitting dejected on a pile of building blocks, scraping the day's caked cement from between his fingers and in his nails. He was still seething and wounded from the discovery of the unfaithfulness of his woman. He exuded wretched animosity. The other workers were keeping their distance. He had been pointed out to Josef, with the caution that he was *anpil deranje* "a bit crazy."

Josef started to sing softly as he approached – the Creole song they had often sung together on the building site in St. Georges:

Pou ale Miami ou bezwen yon paspor
Canada St.Dominigue ou bezwen yon paspor
Min pou ale na siel ou pa bezwen paspor...

Pierre lifted his head and completed the last line,
Se yon sel bagay se asepte Jesus," then he started to cry – not out loud so that Josef could hear it, but in his heart, for the indignities he had endured and the scorn of Robinson, all borne for the love of a woman who had betrayed him. Josef sat down beside him and handed him the work permit. He examined it carefully as Josef explained how he had come by it.

Qu'il aille au diable, "Let him go to hell," Pierre said, as he handed him back the permit. His pride wouldn't allow it. He would stay in Haiti and fight for justice, but he would not go begging on another man's shore again.

They spent some time together chatting and catching up on their respective lives.

Josef left with a promise to hang on to the permit for him, in case he changed his mind.

~~~

Josef and Jacques traveled to Cap Hatien the next morning and spent the night at Claude's house. It was a small, two-roomed concrete house jammed in a row of similar buildings, all of which backed onto the filthy beach behind. The little yard had a fairly decent outhouse and a water tap, which it shared with its two adjoining neighbors.

There was another row of houses between it and the busy street, where Claude's mother lived. She invited them all over for supper, which she had prepared on an open grill outside. They sat half on the street, half in the yard, and visited with the passersby as they ate.

Claude made the most of his last night in Haiti. First he told some tall tales to his three children about life on St. Georges, and how he would send for them all soon. Then he shared some beers with his neighbors, before heading back to his own house to make love to his wife.

~~~

The baggage check at the airport was long and fractious. People argued over their allotted weight and baggage space, the handler insisting on weighing both the passengers and their luggage.

A roar from the vicinity of the runway suddenly diverted everyone's attention. A plane had just started to taxi down the runway when two large pigs had run across the adjoining field and into the plane's path. Two men and a woman had gone out on the runway. In their attempts to round up the pigs, they had confused the beasts entirely. The pigs were now darting about in a crazed zigzag fashion, squealing and grunting as they ran into the direct path of the plane. Wild gesticulations from the ground traffic control officer had alerted the pilot, who had brought the plane to a screeching halt. He opened his door and generally added to the mayhem.

The line at the weigh-in dissipated into a scattered mob that cheered on the spectacle and shouted advice at the hunters.

The pigs would not be herded, the long stretch of flat concrete seeming to hold a fatal attraction for them. As soon as they came near the grass verge, some unseen force would draw them around and back onto the hard hot surface. When it became clear that the pigs had used up their grace time, the owners reluctantly reorganized the chase, this time with machetes. While the pigs had been successful in evading the outstretched grasp of fumbling, slippery human arms, the cold precision of sharpened steel was more accurate. The blades found their marks and wheelbarrows were quickly brought to gather up the hastily butchered carcasses.

Josef's last sight of Haiti before boarding the plane was two young boys scampering off the runway carrying a pig's head between them, an ear firmly grasped in each one's hand. Blood was still dripping from the freshly cut throat, spattering on the boys' ankles as it fell. Their faces were alight with the glee and mischief of an unexpected bounty, which had come their way almost honestly.

CHAPTER 25

Four days of substitute teaching and she had loved every minute of it. In Canada, the experience would have inspired fear and trepidation, as most substitutes are devoured by students who turn into ruthless predators at the first smell of blood. Even the younger grades seem to have a keen sense of their quarry, who is weakened by unfamiliarity with the internal class order. They pounce on the hapless victim with a host of unwritten class rules. "Miss so and so does this and Miss so and so lets us do that."

But these children were so thirsty for knowledge that a teacher who could hardly speak the language was compensated for by the stories she told through her willing interpreter. They were attentive and soaked up her words like dry sponges, which expanded even wider with each piece of encouragement or praise she gave. Most of them were two or three years older than their counterparts in Canada. School here was viewed more as a luxury and privilege than an inalienable right, so some had attended only intermittently, depending on their families' fortunes. Some had transferred from the state-run school in search of a better education. All had come from homes where the fees had been hard-won and there was an expectation of value for money. The nuns had kept the fees to a minimum, and had instituted a series of scholarships to try to hang on to the more promising students. But they badly needed more teachers - ones who would work for little or no pay.

Elizabeth spent Saturday with Gustaf and Marie. They took a picnic up to a mountain stream where there was a popular bathing area. Gustaf, stripped to his boxers, stood on a large rock overhanging a clear, quiet pool that elbowed out from the main stream. He contemplated the drop of about ten feet, telling Elizabeth with great bravado of how he had jumped off it last month with Cheeko. What he neglected to tell her was that Cheeko had fairly pulled him in. The height, now viewed alone, probably looked even more menacing than it had with Cheeko at his side. But Gustaf seemed determined to talk himself into the feat and show Tante Elizabeth just how brave he was.

"He scared," Marie commented, from her secure little rock in the shallows.

"It's okay," Elizabeth told Gustaf. "I'm sure you can do it. But you don't have to do it now, unless you really want to."

"I not scared," he insisted, inching himself closer to the edge. But he sat down on the edge and started to examine the yellow-brown lichen, encrusted on the gray rock.

Elizabeth slid out of her dress and stood in her bra and panties, revealing more of her anatomy than either of them had ever seen before.

"Tante Elizabeth!" Marie squealed. Gustaf sat bolt upright as he tried to appraise the situation. His face registered a combination of horror and glee.

Elizabeth ran to the base of the rock and climbed up beside him. "Come, Gustaf, let's jump together." She grabbed his hand pulling him up. "Okay?"

He nodded and they launched off together, down into the chilling water in a mass of flailing arms and legs. They emerged triumphant, and Gustaf swam to the shore and ran straight back up the slope to repeat the jump. Elizabeth, refreshed and invigorated, lay on a bare slab of rock to dry off and soak up the sun's heat.

Marie came and joined her, examining her rarely exposed belly. "Tante Elizabeth," she confided. "You very white."

~~~

They made their way back to the mission through shaded pathways, leafy quilting softening the earth before them. Life pressed in on the senses, touching them with the sounds and aromas of the dwellings they passed. Drying coffee beans and the essence of orange peel mingled with the cloying drift from the charcoal burners. Distant drums echoed the rhythm of the pulsating forces, which animated the very air they breathed. Elizabeth was alive, her quickened senses capable once again of a full range of feeling. Her toes spread to feel the red earth – powder in the sun-dried stretches, and ooze in gelatinous lumps where the sun had been barred by dense overhang.

Gustaf tapped out a beat with two sticks, answering the call of the drum. Marie timed her steps, moving an untutored body in perfect rhythm with the beat.

That night, Elizabeth prayed for life and the courage to live it to the full.

~ ~ ~

A flat blue sky, sinking its reflection in an untroubled sea, carried the little plane towards the hillocked landscape of St. Georges. Dark blue shattered into white and green where the sea broke over the reef, and the plane swooped low over silver white sands. Talons down, like the osprey that stalked the shores, the plane grabbed its prey, squealing as rubber met concrete in a jarring embrace.

They had repainted the terminal over the summer. Peppermint green and clotted cream replaced the brasher, but battled and peeling, blue and yellow.

"Welcome back, Mrs. Bourke," the immigration officer smiled as she stamped her passport. "How was your summer?"

"It was very nice, thank you." Elizabeth, scanned her name tag, which revealed the name Lightbourne, the name of one of her students. "How is Shanika?" she added.

"She's good. I make her practise her reading all summer."

"Great."

She continued down the line to customs and handed the young man the itemized receipts of her purchases.

"That's okay," he said, beckoning her through. He ignored the thirty dollars in excess of her allowance she was carrying, saving his scrutiny for a more lucrative haul.

Grace stood jiggling at the door, waving her arms and shifting her feet as she tried to get Elizabeth's attention. Ten pounds of summer indulgence bulged over the waist of her tightening blue jeans.

"You look great!" Grace exclaimed when Elizabeth approached. "It's not fair! Look at this," she said, grabbing her waist. "It's all Mary's fault. She's instituted a ladies luncheon once a week and it's doing irreparable damage to my waistline." She hugged her friend and examined her more closely. "You really do look great. I hope you brought some more of that color with you," she said, eyeing the highlights in Elizabeth's hair. "Cause you won't find it here. Meet any rich, handsome, eligible men this summer?" Grace asked, once they were in the jeep.

"Yes, actually," Elizabeth laughed. "But he's not my type."

"Well, you noticed him, didn't you?" Grace needled. "That's a start."

The island was picture-perfect in the midday sun. Generous rainfall had replenished the parched scrub with a green verdure. The salinas were clean-smelling and patrolled by herons hunting for fish in their shallow basins. The houses they passed on Overeast Street were their usual potluck jumble: shabby ones side by side with those proudly painted; rusted, tilting roofs next to straight and shiny.

The road curved and wound its way up the ridge, elevating the land, vista, and people out of the ranks of the ordinary. The little white cottage with the green roof and trim stood straight and proud in its recently manicured yard.

"Home sweet home," Grace cooed as she brought the jeep to a sputtering halt.

"It's good to be back," Elizabeth affirmed. "I know I have some condensed milk, sugar, and coffee in the house. Want to come in?"

"I thought you'd never ask."

The house had been recently cleaned and had a nice, fresh smell. When Elizabeth opened the fridge, she was greeted by fresh fruit and vegetables, milk and bread, and a variety of other groceries. She looked at Grace.

"Guilty," she confessed.

They chatted freely over coffee, Grace bringing Elizabeth up to date with all the goings on, in the white expat community. There had been a number of changes due to end-of-contract turnover. Veronica had left, her husband's position being repatriated to a native Islander. A Scrabble club had been added to the list of things to do. The biggest scandal was that one of the contract officers was having an affair. He was flaunting the relationship in the full light of day and to the disdainful stares of his compatriots. The relationship had caused major ruffles in the social order at first, but people were gradually getting used to the idea and had started to invite them to events as a pair.

"I wouldn't mind," Grace said, "But his wife was out last Christmas and everything seemed hunky-dory. This place will make anyone who stays here on their own eventually crazy. So you can see why I'm worried for your sanity, Elizabeth."

"I've just had the summer off, Grace, so I should be able to stay sane for a few weeks anyway," Elizabeth laughed.

"Okay, but I'm going to keep a close eye on you."

Grace got up and Elizabeth walked with her to the jeep.

"The yard looks really nice," Elizabeth said.

"Yes, Josef is back," Grace said as she swung into her jeep. "And if you don't mind me saying so, honey, he's not your type either."

Elizabeth paled and winced inwardly. She didn't respond.

CHAPTER 26

The long finger of approaching dusk spread shadows across the concrete patio. Elizabeth shifted in the deck chair as the cool evening air whispered across her arms, bumping up her flesh with an unwelcome chill. "It's cold," she complained aloud, rising from the chair and rounding the corner to go back indoors. She had dumped her clothes on the bed and they sat lumped in a pile, creased and bedraggled. She would have to iron them, a task she loathed. She sifted through the pile, casting aside anything that passed scrutiny or that could be concealed from general view. The two shirts she had bought for Josef – one a salmon pink, the other a more conservative blue and gray check – wedged their way into her psyche, allowing bottled thoughts to trickle out.

"Grace is right," she muttered as she started to iron the pink shirt, smoothing out the wrinkles around the collar with care. She forced her memory to replay every distasteful detail of the harsh reality of life on the other side. The physical grind of unrelenting poverty; the sheer and constant effort to keep dirt and despair from swallowing one whole; its haunting presence chewing the mind and spitting it out in a vanquished heap. The sneers and taunts of those guarding the crossing, their fear egged on by ignorance. Their pointing in disgust at the mess, the unsightliness, and general nuisance the burgeoning numbers of trespassers caused. Untutored minds imprisoned within the walls of tradition kept people apart, as firmly as the stanchions between the rungs of a well-built ladder.

"Hello," came a quiet voice from the kitchen door.

She opened the door and invited him in with a wordless gesture of her arm. He stood before her, skin shiny and cold from its recent immersion in the sea, fresh-scented with cologne, and clad in black jeans and a wine-red cotton shirt.

"I missed you," he said softly.

"I missed you, too," she whispered and moved towards him.

They embraced each other tenderly. She felt her body melting against his, seeking refuge from her own fears and uncertainties. His touch remained light, gentle, unsure.

"Elizabeth," he whispered, as he reluctantly released himself from her hold. "I am a small man. I have nothing. It is no good for us."

Tears streamed silently down her face as the terrible truth of his words left their mark. "It's not fair," she choked. But she nodded in agreement.

He kissed her eyelids, wiped her cheeks.

"Come," she said, "I've got something for you." She brought him into the living room, where the pink shirt hung crisp and neat from the back of a chair. "Pour vous," she said, handing it to him.

"It's very nice," he said admiringly. "Thank you, thank you. I have something for you," he said proudly, and he took a small box from his pocket and handed it to her. Inside was a wide-banded pewter bracelet. Images of men and women working on a plantation were engraved in its thick surface; a history lesson of his people in miniature.

"It was my mother's."

"It's beautiful," she said, sliding it over her wrist.

They sat and talked from the heart. They talked of their past loves. They talked in French and English, often understanding only the kernel of each other's words. He told her about Theoline. How he had lost both her and the baby, because he couldn't afford to send them to the hospital. How he would never marry again – unless he could afford to. How it was still painful for him. She told him about Matt and her deep sense of loss. About Michelle and her love for Sam.

Before he left that night, an unspoken covenant had been forged between them. One of the spirit, a space where neither mind nor matter reigned, only the qualities of soul.

CHAPTER 27

October rolled by. Children and schoolwork patterned Elizabeth's life with the simple mosaic of little advances, crises and victories, stitched together with love and diligence like a hand-sewn quilt. Some of her children managed to emerge from the fog with a clearer vision and conquest of the three Rs. Others, she could only provide with a light and a little comfort to make the journey less frightening.

Life on the ridge continued in its well-worn groove. Worlds revolving in their separate orbits, spinning heedless of each other, though their very existence was one of mutual dependence. Bellies filled only when lawns were trimmed and leaves raked. The glow of prosperity and comfort buffed and shined by the phantoms that came and went each day. The little white house with green roof and trim nestled quietly and unobtrusively amongst its neighbors. Josef now tended to the garden and other minor jobs as an act of friendship, not servitude. She fed him whenever she could, always keeping his name in the pot for his unexpected visits – which occurred as often as he could squeeze them in around other work commitments. The biggest luxury she could offer him was a hot shower once a week, as the little house he shared with Jacques had neither water nor electricity.

He now was making regular money, but the demand on it was heavy. There was the work permit and plane ticket – a total of about seven hundred dollars, which Robinson would extract through large docks in pay for the next three months. And his family waited expectantly for whatever he could send back to Haiti. So his overall gain was slight, yet he felt richer and happier than he could remember, and he praised and thanked God every morning and night.

In early November, Elizabeth received a call at school from the harbormaster.

"Miss Elizabeth," he said. "We got a yacht anchored off South Dock. He say he a friend of yours."

"What?"

"Mr. Chrissel, I think."

"Oh, David Cris-tall!" she enunciated slowly.

"Yes Ma'm, I believe so. He will have cleared customs this afternoon, if you want to go check him."

"Thanks, Mr. Smith, I'll come down after school."

~~~

She really didn't want to cycle to South Dock and present herself as the culotted schoolmarm on a bicycle, so she phoned up Grace and asked for a loan of her jeep. She cycled up the ridge in double time, ran into the house, showered, and ransacked her wardrobe for something suitable to wear.

"You are behaving like a complete idiot, Elizabeth Bourke!" she scolded herself, as she rejected the third item she had scrutinized. Finally, she selected cream pants and a hand-painted blouse, dressing quickly to make up for the lost time. A close scrutiny of hair during brushing revealed the unwanted return of gray leaking through the faded auburn highlights. "Damn!"

"Yoo-hoo! Are you there?" came Grace's voice from the kitchen door.

"Yes, come in."

Grace looked at her friend, smiled with a knowing look, and handed her the keys.

"I won't be needing these again until tomorrow morning, so have fun."

"Thanks, Grace."

~~~

The yacht was anchored about two hundred meters from shore. It basked in the afternoon sun, its white hull embraced by turquoise calm waters. Mr. Smith radioed Elizabeth's arrival from shore, and before long David Cristall arrived at the dock, aboard a small dingy. He climbed the stone-cut steps to meet her.

"Elizabeth Bourke." He kissed her on the cheek with the ease of a sophisticate.

"Welcome to St. Georges, David Cristall."

"Do I have time for the grand tour before dinner at a restaurant of your choice?" he asked.

She looked at her watch. "This jeep is on borrowed time, so I will give you the whirlwind tour. Jump in."

"I'm in your hands," he said as he slipped in beside her.

It's funny how quickly one can develop a proprietary pride and allegiance to a place, Elizabeth thought. But that is how she felt about the little island, with its kaleidoscope of people and opinions. She found herself saying "our" and "we" as she described the island. David Cristall, veteran of many a paradise island, listened with deference.

They rattled along in the shockless jeep past the ruins of abandoned salinas, and up along Beach Street where it was clean, prosperous, and painted, the tourist beat. She skirted around Little Haiti and up onto the ridge, finishing the tour at the old lighthouse. They walked along the cliffs and she pointed out the treacherous reefs and the rusting remains of an old cargo ship that had come to grief on them many years ago. He traced his journey for her from the larger Flamingo Island, where he had chartered the yacht to St. Georges, adding that the captain of the charter knew his way around the reefs on all the islands and that he hoped she would join them for the weekend.

They stopped at her house on the way back, and she made reservations for dinner and served them iced tea on the patio.

"It's a nice little house," he offered. "And the view is great. But wouldn't you like to be closer to the sea?"

"Well, yes, but I get all the cooling breezes up here – and, besides, it's what I can afford." She looked at his expensive pants, designer shirt, and the large ring on the middle finger of his right hand and wondered if he actually understood what she meant.

He smiled at her and put his arm lightly on her shoulder. "Ready to eat?" he asked. "I'm really hungry."

~~~

She made a decision before dinner not to have any wine. She wanted to make sure that her response to him was not fueled by alcohol; she already felt nervous and vulnerable. He broke the ice by telling her of an encounter he had with Michelle and Sam at a recent horse show, adding that they both looked well and very happy.

"And how have you been, Elizabeth?" he asked, and she started to relax as they slipped into easy conversation. He slowly drew her into his world, which, he revealed over the course of the evening, was not all glitz and glamour but had been honed by single mindedness and intent. The course had left in its wake the scars of two broken marriages and children that he neither knew nor understood.

She wondered what part of him had been traded for the wealth he had accumulated. He obviously had not lost his love for life nor his ability to focus on and pursue the things he wanted.

She agreed to spend the weekend on the yacht and promised to meet him at eight-thirty the following morning.

~~~

Grace dropped her off at the dock, making full use of the opportunity to size up David Cristall. "Hi, I'm Grace. You know what you're doing?" she asked.

"The captain does," he responded with a smile. "Don't worry, we'll take good care of her."

Elizabeth gave Grace a hug, and they slipped into the waiting dingy and headed out to the yacht.

The decks were of a beautiful teak and ship-shape. The captain, Chris, had a crew of two, so there was no onus on the visitors to actually help. But David was keen to learn and so was put to work on the rigging. Elizabeth decided to explore the boat while it was still moored. It was sixty feet of luxury, with beautifully appointed cabins. She counted four. There were five of them on the cruise, so she hoped that the crew was expected to share.

"Ever sail before, Elizabeth?" asked the captain, who came down to give her an orientation.

"Does a botched attempt at windsurfing on Lake Winnipeg count?" she asked.

"Don't worry, this doesn't capsize. And besides the water is warm here," he laughed. "Just relax and enjoy yourself. The forecast for the next few days is perfect."

"Where do I sleep?" she asked.

"Where do you want to sleep?"

"On my own," she replied.

He looked at her with green, playful eyes. His ruddy broad face was creased from years of sun and sea.

"Here," he said leading her to a cabin that was to the aft of the boat. "This one will have less motion if the waves come up."

"I thought you said the forecast was perfect?"

"It is," he said. "But tonight we'll be crossing a deeper stretch en route to Simpson's Island – our destination for lunch tomorrow."

They set sail under a light but freshening breeze of ten to fifteen knots. The boat skimmed over the surface with ease, and when the sails were trimmed, David came to join her on the fore deck.

"What do you think?" he asked.

"It's wonderful."

"I'm glad you like it,' he said, taking her hand in his. "I try and take at least two or three sailing trips a year. It's my reward to myself for living in Manitoba."

"David, I hope there is no misunderstanding here, but I'm not ready for anything beyond friendship just yet."

"Friendship's fine." He kissed her hand before releasing it. "But please tell when you get beyond "just yet"."

The island looked especially beautiful from the sea. From a distance, the beaches were perfect, unspoiled by litter, and the buildings showed their colors without the imperfections of peeling paint or broken gates.

The boat skirted the island for the first half-hour, and then headed east and out to sea. As they ventured further out the waves increased, but the boat slid over them with ease and Elizabeth stretched out on the deck and let her body sink into the smooth surface, so that she became part of the motion. She had taken to the sailing quite well, having eaten both lunch and supper without any nausea, and had challenged the crew to an after-dinner game of Scrabble. Everybody had participated, and Chris had put the boat on auto-pilot as they headed out across the deep passage towards Simpson's Island.

~~~

Her bunk was comfortable, its lipped side designed to keep bodies secure in a thrashing sea. The wind had slackened, and the roll and yaw of the boat now rocked her gently. Before long she fell asleep.

She had two dreams in quick succession. In the first, there was a group of people singing and clapping their hands. She couldn't actually see them; it was dark, but she was aware of them. Though the lyrics were unclear, sung in some foreign tongue, the theme was sacred and intense. The melody was cut by a cracking noise that seemed to come from above them, and a chilling, inhuman sound followed in its wake. Then silence.

Next a little girl was standing on a mountaintop, looking out to sea. "Maman! Maman!" she cried.

Elizabeth woke up with an acrid taste in the back of her throat. She lurched out of the bunk and wove a disoriented pattern to the steps, grasped the handrail and dragged herself up into the cockpit. Chris was at the helm. He took one look at her staring eyes and green face and put out an arm to steady her as she stumbled towards the side rail. She hung over the edge, retched violently, then lay draped over the side draining her stomach of its fluids. Finally, she sat up. Chris was standing over her with a glass of water and some paper towel in his hand.

"Thanks," she said and she sipped enough water to clear her mouth and throat.

"Feeling better?"

"Much," she replied.

The sea was calm and silver, the moon's muted hues reflecting from the surface. Elizabeth stared into the distance. Out of the blackness appeared a form; shapeless at first, it slowly defined into the silhouette of a sailing vessel. No lights illuminated its mast or defined its bow. It was on a parallel but opposite course, and as it slipped by them in the darkness, its decks leaned heavy with a huddle of silent forms. It disappeared phantom-like as eerily as it had appeared. She might have believed it was an illusion, except that Chris had seen it too. He said nothing. But they exchanged glances and tacitly bound each other to silence. To speak of what they had seen would have bound them to report it.

~~~

Whatever attraction she had found in David Cristall had evaporated with the speed of a Caribbean morning dew. His subtle yet intentioned maneuvers irritated her. His self-assurance, his confidence in his own charm, left her cold. Chris, who made his livelihood not just by sailing, but by maintaining order and harmony in close confines, picked up on Elizabeth's uneasiness.

She confided in Chris that she had made a mistake. That she should never have accepted David's invitation. He set David Cristall to work on all sorts of navigational tasks, stroking his ego with much encouragement and some responsibility.

By the time they returned to shore and it was time to say goodbye, David was in flying form – oblivious of his negative effect on Elizabeth, and delighted with his sailing prowess. She could hardly wait to see the back of him and was greatly relieved to wave off the yacht as it headed seaward.

When she reached home there was a plastic bag of fruit hanging from the kitchen doorknob.

CHAPTER 28

The trip with David Cristall established two things in Elizabeth's consciousness; she was starting to feel whole again; and with that wholeness came the strength to function independently, as a single person. He had caused her to examine her singleness and she found that it was, for now, quite okay. She wanted someone she could share simple intimacies with, who did not demand to consume her in the exchange.

And that she found was the great joy she shared with Josef. Their relationship was not sustained by the sweeping passions of the more primal forces that bring a man and woman together, but rather through a caring that manifested itself in little deeds and acts – such as the bag of fruit that she found on her return from the sailing trip. Sometimes they shared the details of their separate lives. Like when Michelle wrote to say that she and Sam hoped to get married in the summer, and that Mrs. Ketner loved her. Or when Josef's brother bought a car and was starting his own taxi service. But mostly they shared the little pleasures and burdens of everyday life: an especially beautiful island sunset, a leaky roof, or a new song.

~ ~ ~

The letter came as a shock, but its ominous content was a dread she had already anticipated. Somewhere in the deep recesses of her mind, it had skulked like a chained dog waiting to snap at her in moments of unexpected quiet, or in her sleep. It was simple and to the point: the blood tests had come back and Marie was HIV positive. She had had a return of a respiratory infection and was once again laid low. Françoise was still in Gonaives, her own family problems spinning a burdensome web around her already complicated life.

Elizabeth's decision was immediate and without hesitation: she would give up her job in St. Georges and go to Haiti to be with Marie for as long as she was needed. It was not born out of pity, or even compassion, but of love for the little girl whose gentle soul and keen mind had firmly established a place in her heart.

Mrs. Clark was genuinely moved by the fate of Marie, and sorry to see Elizabeth go. Grace thought she was plain crazy. (But she had questioned Elizabeth's sanity after she had reiterated her firm conviction that David Cristall was positively and absolutely not her type. And her curious relationship with the Haitian laborer totally baffled her.) Still, she loved her. She got the expats to throw her a party, at which they presented her with a suitcase full of hardly-worn children's clothes and a generous check to help with medical expenses.

Of all of her friends, Josef alone came closest to understanding the nature of her decision. He sat out on the patio with her, running his fingers over the difficult script as she translated the words. His eyes bore testament to a shared pain.

"What you do now?" he asked.

"I will go to her."

"You go, Elizabeth. She need you, she love you."

And they sat in silence for a long time, and then he started to sing.

~~~

They spent one last evening together before she left.

"Let's go fish," he suggested, and they headed off down the donkey trail that led to the beach.

His stash of hooks and lines were where he had left them, though he had not been fishing for a long time. There was two hours of light left and the sun hung suspended between heaven and earth, a crimson disc slipping slowly off its flawless blue canvas. They made their way onto the reef to repeat the process that had first cemented their friendship. There was neither tension nor empty space between them. It was a quiet space, cut only by the swish of their lines as they worked the reef, coaxing it to give up some of its bounty.

"That's good," he said after landing a handsome marbled grouper. "Let's go."

They walked across the jagged reef and onto the soft sand,

now taupe under the setting sun. His long, loping stride created a gap between them, and he stopped to wait. She took his hand, and they both exhaled and quietly continued on their way.

As they approached the donkey path, they saw a woman and her child making their way onto the beach. The clasp of their hands momentarily weakened, threatening to fall into the deep divide like a swinging bridge cut from its moorings. Their touch loosened, from a clasp to fingers flat on fingers and then tightened again as their fingers slid and intertwined, firm in the knowledge that the bridge that joined their different worlds was secure.

THE END

…...Since We have created you all from the same substance it is incumbent on you to be even as one soul, to walk with the same feet, eat with the same mouth and dwell in the same land, that from your inmost being, by your deeds and actions, the signs of oneness and the essence of detachment may be made manifest.
-Bahá'u'lláh

ISBN 1553696808